Rebecca Barrett

Callahan on the Case

Secret Staircase Books

Cat Callahan Mysteries
by Rebecca Barrett and Susan Yawn Tanner

Callahan on the Case
Callahan and the Horses of Hope
(and more coming soon!)

Callahan's Christmas Feast (short story)
A Callahan Christmas (short story)

Rebecca Barrett

Callahan on the Case

Cat Callahan Cozy Mysteries, Book 1

Callahan on the Case
Published by Secret Staircase Books, an imprint of
Columbine Publishing Group LLC
PO Box 416, Angel Fire, NM 87710

Book layout and design by Secret Staircase Books
Illustrations by Becky's Graphic Design, Svetlana Dubovetcaia,
Oxilixo, Georgesheldon, Bustiuc Dumitru

First e-book edition: January, 2024
First paperback edition: January, 2024

Publisher's Cataloging-in-Publication Data

Barrett, Rebecca
Callahan on the Case / by Rebecca Barrett.
p. cm.
ISBN 978-1649141576 (paperback)
ISBN 978-1649141583 (e-book)

1. Cat Callahan (Fictitious character)—Fiction. 2. Mystery—
Fiction. 3. Amateur sleuths—Fiction. 4. Animals in mystery fiction.
I. Title

Cat Callahan Mystery Series, Book 1.
Barrett, Rebecca, Cat Callahan Cozy Mysteries.

BISAC : FICTION / Mystery.

813/.54

*In memory of the "original" Daxter, cat-about-town.
And for Teagan Toifel.*

Acknowledgements

No story is perfect without the attention to detail that a wonderful group of beta readers can bring to a project. In *Callahan on the Case*, those readers were: Marcia Koopmann, Susan Gross, Sandra Anderson, Paula Webb, Isobel Tamney, Amy Connolley, Donna Townsend, Georgia Ryle, Eve Osborne, Dawn Hasiotis, and Tammy Baughman. Many thanks to each and every one of them.

Chapter One

Life is full of wonders. Take potted meat, for example. If you've never tried it, don't knock it. I only wish I'd known about it sooner in life. I suppose the lack of an opposable thumb comes into play but still, I'm happy to have finally discovered this delicacy. The saltine crackers add a nice something to the mix.

I'm not the only one who likes life's simple pleasures. My newfound friend seems to have enjoyed his portion just as much as I did. Now we're both enjoying the sun here on the patio that connects the guest house and the servants' quarters of FDR's Little White House. It's a pleasant spring day in Warm Springs and I won't deny being on the verge of a nap when my companion speaks.

"So, what's your name?"

I open my eyes to see who he's talking to. There's no one around.

He scratches me behind the ear. "You can call me Dax. Short for Daxter."

I stare at him. Does he seriously think I'm going to answer?

"Don't give me that Dirty Harry dead eye. Just trying to be sociable."

He falls silent. I wait but it seems he's done. Then he speaks again.

"What *should* I call you?" *He cocks his head to one side and studies me.*

I don't know if that That Darn Cat really qualifies as a name but people seem to use it a lot in my presence. How to relay this bit of information to my companion is a mystery so I keep silent.

"I'll call you Harry. Or Callahan."

We stare at each other.

"Yeah, I think you're a Callahan. You got the stare down cold."

He takes a beat-up paperback out of his knapsack and settles more comfortably against the wall of the garage of the servants' quarters. But he can't seem to settle to the story.

He closes the book. "A fan of FDR, are you?" *he asks.*

To be truthful, I've never given the thirty-second president much thought. The only reason I'm here on the museum grounds is a severe case of boredom. Warm Springs is a nice enough place, I grant you, but aside from the recent demise of The Annoying Rooster, not much happens. I suppose I'm feeling a little restless.

However, the people of Warm Springs seem inordinately fond of FDR. Or at least his memory, seeing as how he's dead and all that. The degree to which he's revered might make you think he had nine lives, but, no. He was a mere human.

When Dax gets no response from me, he pulls his baseball cap low on his forehead and leans against the wall again. I watch him for a moment and decide he's finally ready to settle in for a bit of a snooze. I close my eyes and drift to the edge of sleep and then a scream rips through the air, sending me up the dogwood tree in a flash.

Children aren't my thing. Noisy little brats. They're tolerable, I suppose, from a distance.

Which is exactly what I aim to do … distance myself from this pack who have descended on our quiet little corner of the museum grounds. I want to be well out of reach before they decide that rolling down a grassy slope toward a straight drop down the mountain isn't entertaining enough. I'm not THAT bored.

Dax seems to share my opinion of the situation. He returns his paperback to the knapsack and shoulders it as he ambles off down the driveway of the Little White House, away from the main buildings of the compound and the little delinquents.

The Red Head is the leader. He's showing off for the little girl underneath my tree with a Scottish terrier sitting at her feet. I know this dog. And the girl. They're regulars at the ice cream parlor at the Warm Springs Bed & Breakfast.

None of Red Head's efforts to make her smile are working. I guess I have to give him credit for effort. That said, I'll climb another branch higher. In my experience, the attention span in males of this age is about that of a gnat. I don't plan to be his next challenge.

It's beyond me why humans bother to drag their offspring to places like a museum before the age of adulthood. Maybe if it was Teddy Roosevelt they were studying, all that Rough Riders and bear hunting. What would it have been like to have explored the Wild West? These boys are probably no more than eight or nine, an age when the significance of FDR's Little White House is a bore. Especially since, I believe, school will be out in a few short days. Who in their right mind would think these knuckleheads would learn anything with the freedom of summer within reach?

I think they've tired of playing at Federal agents shooting assassins trying to storm the doors of the Little White House. One races across the drive toward the slope up to the servants' cottage near where I perch. The Red Head brandishes the bit of tree branch he's using as an imaginary gun at his companions-in-terror as he turns to stand his ground at the door to the garage beneath the living quarters.

A woman comes hurrying from the direction of the administration building higher on the hill. She arrives on the spot just in time to prevent the troops from storming up the stairs to the servants' apartment in their game. She looks familiar.

She pushes an errant blonde curl back from her face. "Where are your parents?" *she asks as she physically blocks the doorway.*

The Red Head is the leader. He glances in the direction of the little girl to see if she's watching. He steps forward. "We want to go up."

"I'm sure you do. But you can only go with adult supervision."

"We don't need supervision." *He puffs out his chest, the challenge clear in his eyes.*

Ha. The little gangster is gutsy.

The blonde, obviously an employee of the museum, tries to hide her amusement.

Down the slope from this standoff, the front door of the Little White House opens and two women step out. The taller of them looks up the incline and sees the confrontation.

"Hannah!"

The blonde turns, shades her eyes against the angle of the sun, and smiles. "Jackie! I didn't know you had arrived."

This Jackie person hurries up the walkway to the servants' quarters, her companion at her heels. They catch the blonde called Hannah up in a three-way hug as they jump up and down and squeal like little kids.

"Oh, Hannah! It's so good to see you!" *Jackie is grinning*

from ear to ear.

"I've been looking forward to this week. Why didn't you ask for me at the admissions office?" *Hannah's cheeks are pink with excitement. The smile on her face changes her attractive features into something of a knockout.*

"We knew you were working and didn't want to disrupt your day. Besides, it's been ages since I took the tour of the site."

The little boys begin sword fighting on the bricked patio that connects the guest quarters and the servants' quarters. Hannah sighs. "Excuse me for a moment."

She shushes the boys and with hands on hips, demands, again, to know where their parents are.

The gang of four look at each other and shrug.

"Well, I guess you'll just have to wait for them at the admissions office with me. Surely they'll come looking for you at some point." *She takes her cell phone out and presses a button.* "Oscar, could you join me at the guest house, please?" *She puts the phone back into the pocket of her skirt, stares the boys down, and says,* "Don't move."

The moment Hannah turns back to her friends, the quartet sprints toward the guard houses further up the rise, over the bumper gates, and are last seen racing toward the Avenue of the States' Stones.

Hannah sighs and laughs. "I'll have to send Oscar after them."

"They're just being boys," *Jackie says.*

"I know, and I hate to have to discipline them, but this is a museum and it's my job. It's one thing to enjoy the outdoor elements but they were getting out of hand. A tourist stopped in the office to complain that they were going to fall off the mountain. And, as usual, the parents are nowhere to be found." *She gives a wave of her hand.* "But forget about them. Come on and let's have some tea." *As she links her arm with Jackie, she notices the little girl and the dog.*

"Teagan, I didn't know you were down here." *She motions for her to come forward.* "You remember my sorority sisters, don't you? Jackie and Phyllis?"

Ah. Now I remember. The little blonde belongs to the adult blonde. I've seen them around town together. With the dog.

Teagan smiles shyly but says nothing.

"We're going to my office to have tea and make plans for our weekend. Want to help us?"

Teagan looks at Hannah then up the tree to where I'm perched.

"Ah," *says Hannah.* "It's That Darn Cat."

"Well," *she continues,* "you and Fergus can stay here but don't tease him."

Fergus. What kind of name is that for a dog? Obviously, he doesn't seem to mind as his ears perk up and he wags his short tail. Dogs are so easy.

I hope he and Teagan don't think I'm here for their amusement. The female of the species is even more inexplicable than male humans so I'll keep my distance.

Hannah and her friends head up the hill toward the main building of the museum complex, talking over each other in their excitement of being together. I climb a branch higher as Fergus barks. He doesn't seem particularly friendly.

No sooner than Hannah and company are out of sight, the gang of pre-adolescent males reappear like a locust plague.

The Red Head has a look of purpose in his eyes. Denied the stairwell a few minutes earlier by the park ranger, Hannah, he has returned with his motley crew to storm the servants' cottage.

As the boys clatter up the wooden steps, the Scottish terrier rises to his feet, his body aquiver with indignation. Not bad for a dog, I suppose.

The little girl, Teagan, stands her ground for a moment longer until the cries of victory from the boys change to a note of surprise, then anger.

"Hey, you!" *It's the voice of the Red Head.* "You can't take a nap here!"

Another juvenile male shouts, "I'm telling!"

Teagan and the terrier run up the stairs as one of the boys comes clattering down. With a quick look over his shoulder, he races off in the direction of the main building of the museum.

A sharp bark from the terrier brings me down from my perch high in the dogwood as two more boys rush down the steps. Obviously, it's time for cool heads to prevail. Mine, of course.

The moment I cross the threshold of the doorway leading onto the stairs, I know something foul is afoot. This could be interesting. A bit of excitement in little old Warm Springs.

At the top of the stairs is a small living room with a pot-bellied stove, a small kitchen annex, and two bedrooms. All the rooms off the living room have a see-through barrier to keep tourists out. Here I find Teagan, the Red Head, and Fergus staring into one of the bedroom displays. In plain sight is a man lying on the bed on his side, facing away from us toward the far wall. A dark stain on the pillow tells the tale.

"He's not supposed to be there. No one is supposed to be there," *the Red Head protests indignantly.*

Teagan is quiet for a moment. Her gaze travels over the surface of the protective barrier. "How did he get in?"

I look up at her with a smidgen of admiration. If she isn't a cool one. And sharp. A budding junior detective, perhaps? She's correct in her observation. There's no way to get into the protected area. The barrier is floor to ceiling so not even I could slither over or under it. And I have been known to get into some tight places in my time. So, how did the killer get the body into the room?

I sniff along the floorboard. It's a custom fit. Designed, no doubt, to not only keep foot traffic out, but to preserve the old furnishings from the elements of Georgia's often muggy weather and various insects and rats. Surely there's some way for the rangers who work at the museum complex to gain access.

Ah, the wood frame of the clear material is hinged, like any ordinary door, but there's no doorknob.

Adult voices signal the approach of Hannah and a male. The chatter of high-pitched pre-pubescent boys vies for supremacy. The cavalry has arrived.

* * *

"How could this happen, Oscar? How did he get in there?" Hannah Sanderson schooled her voice to hide the panic she felt. The man lying in the middle of a museum display was definitely dead. If the lack of movement from their attempts to get his attention wasn't enough, the dark reddish stain on the pillow confirmed his status.

"Why are you asking me? I'm not in charge of the displays." Oscar was clearly distancing himself from any responsibility for a breach in the museum's security. "All I do is keep an eye on the tourists when we're open."

Hannah had her cell phone out and had already punched in the number for Warm Springs Police Department. Clay Bishop answered the phone and Hannah mentally rolled her eyes. The patrolman had been trying to get her to go out with him for several months. He was good looking and knew it. Her refusals had only increased his determination.

"Hi, Clay, it's Hannah over at the museum."

"Well, hello, Hannah. Change your mind about the Memorial Day picnic?"

"We have a dead body at the museum."

Clay chuckled.

"No, seriously, Clay. There's a dead body on the bed in the servants' quarters above the garage. I think there's blood."

She heard the change in his voice.

"Are you sure?"

"Well, no. I mean he might be alive but he's not moving. He doesn't respond when we call out to him."

"Have you checked for a pulse?"

"No, Clay. He's behind the Plexiglass barrier. We're waiting for someone to bring the key down here." She hesitated. "But I think he's dead. There's something about the stillness, you know? I can't explain it."

"Right. I'll be there in ten minutes. I'll have Patti call an ambulance. Don't open the display until I get there."

* * *

Scoop Russell was at his desk in Atlanta, browsing through a brochure on deep sea fishing off the coast of Cancun, Mexico when he got the call. The Warm Springs Police Department had a dead body right smack dab in the middle of the FDR state museum. In a sealed room. A real Agatha Christie whodunnit.

His gaze dropped down to the bottom of the brochure and the deadline for cancellation. He had three days. Doable, he decided. How complicated could it be in a small town like Warm Springs, Georgia?

He lifted the receiver of his desk phone and dialed. Birdie answered on the second ring.

"Saddle up, Birdie. We're off to Warm Springs."

"Yeah? What's the case? Accident? Poachers?

Vandalism?"

"Colonel Parker in the pantry with the cleaver."

"Murder?"

"In a locked room, no less."

"Hot dog!"

"I'm glad you find your work so rewarding."

"A locked room, Scoop! This is what every forensic scientist dreams of."

"Well, stop dreaming and assemble the team. See what kind of accommodations are available in Warm Springs. Get as near the museum grounds as you can. We have to wrap this up in two days."

"Ah. Fishing over the Memorial Day weekend?"

"Better than that. Deep sea fishing off the coast of Cancun."

The team consisted of Scoop, Birdie, and McFadden. As the lead on the case, Scoop felt the talents of the three of them would be sufficient to wrap things up quickly.

Accommodations were an issue in the small town. Since it was crucial to be as close to the museum as possible, Birdie booked them into the Hotel Warm Springs, a bed and breakfast in the heart of the small business district.

The hour drive from Atlanta to Warm Springs took an hour and a half. Late afternoon traffic on I-85 was a beast. Scoop drove straight through the crossroads of the town's business district on Highway 27 to the turn-off onto Little White House Road.

Two patrol cars and a hearse sat in the parking lot at the end of the long, winding lane that led to the secluded complex that had been President Franklin Delano Roosevelt's retreat. There were three additional cars parked together well away from the main museum building. One had a government-issue tag. The staff, Scoop decided.

A patrolman stood at the top of the steps leading up from the parking lot to the entrance to the museum compound. A little girl sat one step up from the bottom of the stairs. A black Scottie sat at her feet.

As he approached, the child looked up and squinted at him as she pushed a strand of long blonde hair behind her ear.

"Are you the FBI?" she asked.

"No. I'm Scoop Russell with the Georgia Department of Natural Resources Law Enforcement team." He took his identification badge from his pocket and solemnly showed it to her. "You were expecting the FBI?"

"It's a dead body. He was murdered."

"Yeah? How do you know he was murdered?"

"The room can only be locked from the outside."

"I see."

The police officer made his way down the steps just as Birdie joined Scoop and the little girl.

"Who's this?" Birdie set her heavy crime scene bag on the bottom step and put her hand out to the Scottie to sniff.

"That's Fergus." The little girl stood.

"And what's your name?"

"Teagan."

The policeman broke in. "She's the assistant director's daughter." He looked from Birdie to Scoop. "You're the team sent to deal with the body?"

"That would be us. Scoop Russell." Scoop shook hands with the patrolman. "This is Birdie and bringing up the rear," he glanced over his shoulder at the third member of their team crossing the parking lot, weighed down with various cases of equipment, "is McFadden."

"Clay Bishop," the officer replied. "I was the first on the scene."

"Who discovered the victim?"

"A bunch of kids."

All eyes went to Teagan. The terrier stood and moved closer to her, his body aquiver from nose to tail.

Scoop crouched to bring himself down to Teagan's level. "Well, now, I can see why you were expecting the FBI." He glanced up at Clay Bishop then returned his attention to the little girl. "Where's your dad?"

She buried her fingers in the dog's hair. "He's dead."

"I thought—" He looked up at the patrolman.

"Her mother, Hannah Sanderson, is the assistant director."

Scoop felt the anger rising but he kept his voice calm as he spoke to the child. "How did you find the body?"

"It was the other kids. The tourists. They were playing at sword fighting and ran up the stairs to the servants' quarters. They thought the man was sleeping."

"But you didn't?"

"No."

"Why's that?"

She thought about it a minute. "He didn't move." She kneaded the dog's fur with one hand as he leaned into her body. "You could tell he wasn't breathing."

Scoop had received only the broad strokes of the scene with the initial phone call. Had there been blood? He had been afraid of what the child might have seen. But stillness, that was a very discerning observation.

Clay Bishop seemed to appreciate that he was losing ground with the investigative team. He cleared his throat.

"We took statements from everyone who was in the park at the time. Got all their contact details. Shirley's going through the receipts for the day, checking credit cards to identify folks who were in here earlier. So far, we've only found three who paid with cash."

The door of the museum opened and a brunette stepped through with a large gray cat with droopy ears following at her heels. "Teagan! Your mother is looking all over for you." She hurried down the steps. "You were supposed to wait—" The brunette stopped as her gaze fell on Scoop. As she continued on down the steps, she said, "You were supposed to wait in the office with Shirley."

"She was busy."

"Oh, sweetie." She hugged the child to her and turned to Scoop and his entourage. "Jackie," she said. "Jackie Harper. I'm a friend of Hannah's, in town for the weekend." She gestured toward the main building. "You'll find her inside to the right. She's expecting you."

"Thanks." Scoop started up the steps and Teagan tried to fall in step with him.

Jackie held her back. "No, sweetie. You need to stay with me."

"But I found the body." Teagan protested.

"I know, sweetie, but Oscar and your mother can show them where."

"They need to take my statement."

"Officer Bishop already took your statement."

The look of disappointment in her expression made Scoop stop for a moment. "Tell you what, Teagan. When we've had a chance to look things over, I'll review your statement with you. I wouldn't want to miss any important details."

She sighed, then reluctantly nodded her head.

As he continued up the steps, he could feel the gaze of the brunette boring into the back of his head. He looked over his shoulder and she quickly lowered her gaze to the child.

Chapter Two

*O*dd. Not only did the sorority sister called Jackie react to the new law in town but Hannah Sanderson looks as though the arrival of Scoop Russell is the last straw. Her cheeks flushed a bright pink as she looked up at the sound of her office door opening. Quickly she glanced away with a short, sharp inhalation of breath.

Who is this guy? And why is everyone reacting so strongly to him? He appears oblivious to the stir his appearance on the scene has created among the females, including the little girl. Not sure what this says about his detecting skills. I, on the other hand, miss nothing. I thought he handled the screw-up about Teagan's father well, leading me to believe he knows his stuff. Am I wrong?

Teagan's reaction to Scoop's arrival is understandable. She sees him as the posse riding to the rescue. The lawman who will untangle the mystery of the dead body in the sealed room. A comrade in arms.

And if I'm not mistaken, hope beats in her little heart that he will let her in on solving the puzzle. I suspect a born detective's instinct will override any fear of a dead body and the puzzle of who and how will be the guiding force for her. I'll take her under my wing. Never let it be said that Callahan let a fertile young mind go to waste. Callahan. Yeah, I like the sound of that. Cat Callahan. Has a nice ring to it if I do say so myself.

Jackie and Hannah's reaction to Scoop is another puzzle. Surprise with perhaps a touch of worry on Jackie's part. More of a kick in the gut on Hannah's part.

I'll figure out the cause of this odd behavior eventually but for now, I'll take my own measure of the man. Let the game begin.

"Scoop Russell." *He extends his hand.* "Critical Incident Response Team."

Hannah rises from her chair. "Yes." *She shakes the offered hand.* "About the body."

Scoop's eyebrows shoot up and a hint of a smile passes quickly. "Yes. About the body."

The color deepens in Hannah's face and neck and she glances away from his direct gaze. "Sorry. New territory for me."

"An understandable reaction." *Scoop nods toward the open door behind him.* "My team is here to process the scene. Is there someone who can show us the way?"

Hannah comes from behind the desk. "Follow me."

It's interesting to see how an unexpected dead body affects the average human. Hannah's reaction is certainly understandable. I doubt she's ever seen a murder victim before. Then there's Oscar. You can read his body language as we approach. Standing guard at the bottom of the stairs leading up to the crime scene has him as spooked as a cat in a room full of rocking chairs. I know, I know, a tired old pun but in this case appropriate. He keeps glancing around as if an axe murderer is going to materialize out of thin air.

Oscar may be just the ticket for keeping unruly children in line, but he'd never be anyone's second in command. Fortunately, he ignored me earlier which allowed me to thoroughly inspect the crime scene and the immediate surroundings.

Scoop Russell, on the other hand, has an easy confidence about him that suggests he knows a thing or two about high crimes and misdemeanors. A real Cool Hand Luke attitude, that one. We'll see. There are things I need to show him. If he's as quick as I hope he is, he'll follow my lead.

* * *

Scoop and his team had followed Hannah through the Legacy Exhibit, past the Unfinished Portrait of FDR that he had been sitting for when he suffered the cerebral hemorrhage that ended his life.

A fitting way to die, Scoop thought, in the place he loved so well, among people who, in turn, loved him dearly. He wondered what that must be like as he followed the path of the huge gray cat with strange droopy ears that had taken the forward point on their advancement toward a very nervous, slightly overweight man at a building that Scoop assumed housed the servants' quarters.

As soon as they stepped off the road to cut across the patch of lawn that led up to the entrance, the fidgety ranger spoke. "Can I leave now? It's long past quitting time and my wife's expecting me for supper."

"Oscar, this is the investigative team from Atlanta." Hannah indicated Scoop with a slight lift of her chin in his direction. "The lead investigator, Scoop Russell. He might have some questions for you before you go."

"But I don't know anything!"

Scoop stepped forward and extended his hand in greeting.

After a slight hesitation, Oscar shook it.

"I appreciate you going beyond the call of duty, Oscar. It's not every day we ordinary folks find ourselves with a dead body on our hands, am I right?"

Oscar cleared his throat and made an aww-shucks bob of his head. "Kinda unexpected, that's for sure."

"Well, I sure appreciate you keeping a close eye on the scene. I wouldn't want to keep you any longer so if you'll give me your number and address, maybe we can meet up a little later. How's that sound?"

"Sure. Fine." Oscar was warming to Scoop. "I suppose I could stay a bit longer if you need me to."

"That's awful good of you, Oscar, but we're going to be here a while." Scoop took a notebook from his coat pocket and looked at Oscar expectantly.

Oscar cleared his throat again and rattled off his number and address.

"Great," Scoop said as he returned the notebook to his pocket. "You go on home and I'll ring you up to get your insights into the situation later."

"Sure thing, Mr. Russell."

"Call me Scoop."

"Okay. Scoop. Just give a holler if you need anything."

"Will do."

From the corner of his eye, Scoop could see the beginnings of a grin on Birdie's face. He clapped Oscar on the back as he turned him in the direction of the main building of the museum.

Oscar brought his hand toward his forehead in an almost salute and headed up the rise. Scoop watched him top the hillock leading away from the servants' quarters. Finally, he turned his attention to the entrance of the stairwell. His team, from long practice, stood patiently waiting while Scoop let his gaze travel over the small building that was anchored to his left by an almost identical structure.

It appeared that the only means of access to the living quarters was up the interior stairs located on the left side of the building. There were small windows above but they could only be reached with a ladder. The double doors of the garage that occupied the bottom floor on the west end of the building were secured by a substantial padlock.

His gaze fell to the gray cat sitting on the third step. "The proverbial museum cat?" he asked.

Hannah glanced at the cat and shook her head. "No. He's a stray. I guess you could say he belongs to the town. I've never seen him on the museum grounds before."

"Has he been near the body?"

Clay cleared his throat. "He was up there earlier but I shooed him away."

Scoop grunted. "Keep that in mind, Birdie."

"Yeah, Boss," she replied as she followed him up the narrow steps.

At the top of the stairs, Scoop repeated the careful scrutiny of the scene from the small landing. Birdie and McFadden lined the narrow stairwell behind him, patiently waiting.

Scoop looked down and saw the gray cat sitting at his feet, for all the world mimicking his behavior.

"Scat!"

The cat twitched a scarred right ear as if to discourage an annoying fly.

Scoop called down to Clay. "You want to corral this cat

and get him out of the middle of the crime scene?"

"That Darn Cat," Clay said under his breath as he squeezed past Birdie and McFadden to reach the landing. He caught the cat around his mid-section and brought him to cradle against his chest.

The cat went willingly enough. As the patrolman turned to head down the stairs, the cat looked over his shoulder at Scoop who could have sworn the look on the feline's face was one of disbelief.

Everyone's a critic, thought Scoop, before focusing on the scene before him.

There was a scuff mark on the wood of the threshold. A drag mark, perhaps. Made by the victim or by the police and museum staff when they opened the display door? Would the policeman know?

Thus far, Scoop was not impressed with the local law. Their preservation of the scene was certainly suspect.

* * *

Clay handed the cat to Hannah as she waited on the small brick patio. The cat accepted this state of affairs, seemingly content to nestle in Hannah's arms as she scratched behind his ears. In short order, he began to purr.

"He likes you," Clay said. He grinned. "He has good taste."

Hannah smiled but her thoughts were upstairs with the investigative team. More specifically, they were with Scoop Russell. She was trying to decide how she felt about her old heartthrob showing up on her turf. Not that he had ever known about the intense attraction she had suffered through her freshman year at university.

She had barely registered with him back then. If not for her brother being on the baseball team, their paths might never have crossed. It was obvious he had no memory of her.

Did that hurt? Well, maybe it stung her pride a bit. But she felt nothing else, she was sure of that.

Clay, who stood to her right, gave her a gentle nudge with his elbow. When she looked up at him, he grinned again and winked.

Why couldn't she respond to his interest? He was good looking enough with his wholesome, crew-cut, just enough muscle, and a winning smile. And even though he was a little vain about those looks, he was kind, funny, and easy to be around.

The problem, she knew, was that she didn't feel that rush of anticipation, that sense of breathlessness that Scoop had created that long ago first year of college. Nor did she feel the all-encompassing love and desire that, years later, a mere glance from David had evoked.

Scoop had been the wild, impetuous longing of summer wine, an intense, hormonally driven desire that only youth can experience. David had been bigger than life, exciting, fearless. He had stolen her heart on their first date.

But David had always been chasing the next adventure. In that moment Hannah realized that Scoop and David were one and the same. She had a type.

She looked away from the question in Clay's eyes and focused her attention on the cat.

Chapter Three

Well, there's no doubt that the CIRT crew is thorough. After kicking me out of the crime scene, Scoop spent about ten minutes up there but has since been wandering about the courtyard and the neighboring guest house. His team is still at it with the body and the apartment. The one called McFadden comes down the stairs and brings a camera with a serious looking lens attached. He begins taking photos of the exterior of the building, the garage, up the pathway down which we came. Very thorough, indeed.

Scoop stands in the doorway of the guest house on the far side of the patio, surveying the lay of the land, his gaze traveling over the rise before him. Now, he crosses back to where Hannah stands with me in her arms and scratches me under my chin. Perhaps he has had a change of heart about my participation.

"Hannah," *he says.* "As in Hannah Wilson?"

A blush heightens the color in her cheeks. "Yes. I'm surprised you remembered."

"It's the eyes. You've got Eddie's eyes. So does your little girl."

Scoop turns to Clay. "Anyone know who the victim is?"

"A reporter of some kind. Shirley remembers him trying to chat her up several days ago about the Roosevelt family."

"Shirley?"

"She runs the museum shop, mans the ticket desk sometimes. Said he spent a good bit of time browsing, but in the end didn't buy anything."

"Did she remember a name?"

"Something Frenchie, she thinks. Said she's seen him in town. Thinks he was staying at the B&B, maybe."

"Frenchie?"

"Yeah. One of those names with a de before it, like DeVille or D'Olive. Something like that."

"Did he have an accent?"

"No. Just the unusual name."

Now we're getting somewhere. Our victim is a stranger in town. That changes things. Why would a local kill a stranger? I'll have to find this Shirley and see what's what. Everyone talks to shop keepers, especially in the South.

The hotel is where the case is taking us. I'll have to get into the Frenchie's room and see what I can learn from his belongings. The inn keeper should be able to give us the dirt on our mystery man. What's her name? I should remember. What I do remember is the tempting smell of fresh waffle cones in the air when I curled up in the mail truck for a snooze. Gerrie… That's it. Gerrie runs the hotel and the ice cream shop next door. Her fresh peach ice cream is calling my name. Now that's what I call killing two birds with one stone, fresh peach ice cream and a puzzle to solve.

Scoop puts his hands in his pants pockets and stares off down the mountain in the direction of the Little White House. Finally, he turns to Clay. "Do you have a map of the museum complex? Any alternate means of access other than the public road? The layout of the buildings?"

"Sure. The museum has a site map but I'm thinking you want something more detailed? Trails and things you won't find with Google."

"You'd be thinking right."

"Billy Brad is up in the office helping Shirley go through receipts. I'll send him to the station to see what he can put together for you."

"That'd be a big help."

Clay looks from Scoop to Hannah and back again. His eyes close to half-mast and he gives a hint of a nod, a kind of a-ha gesture, before he turns toward the main building of the museum.

Scoop watches Clay head on over the rise toward the office then turns to Hannah. "So, how about the guided tour of the grounds."

She puts me down. "I'll need to go to the office and get my keys."

"Just the grounds for now. I need to see the layout first hand. It helps me see the big picture.

"Sure." *Hannah cuts across the grassy slope, passing the entrance to the garage beneath the living quarters, and toward the curving drive beyond.*

As Scoop follows, I begin to twine between his legs.

* * *

"Scat!" Scoop said to his nemesis, as he'd begun to think of the gray cat, caused him to misstep.

"Here," Hannah bent down to gather the cat in her arms, "let me hold him."

But the feline nuisance was in no mood to be accommodating. He scooted out of Hannah's reach only to return to impeding Scoop's attempt to navigate the slope down to the roadway. The cat was like a matador feigning in one direction then the other as he thwarted Scoop's forward movement.

"What the devil's wrong with him?" Scoop stopped in his tracks and watched as the cat did a little stand-off then scurried to the corner of the building by the garage doors, sat down, and looked back expectantly.

Hannah walked toward him. "I think he wants to show you something."

"Like a feline Lassie?"

The cat flicked his right ear. A sign of annoyance, Scoop thought, then grinned at such a fanciful notion.

"He's probably found a mouse or a dead bird," Scoop said as he joined Hannah at the corner of the garage.

But there, caught on one of the overlapping clapboards was a small piece of dark cloth. Scoop squatted to examine the fabric. It was clearly torn from a heavy-duty piece of material, and recently. There was no evidence of weathering from the elements.

"Well, well." Scoop scratched the cat behind his ear. "What have we here?" He glanced at Hannah and raised his hand. "Stay there. We need to check this area for any shoeprints or other signs of disturbance." He rose and carefully guided Hannah as he retraced their steps. He gave a sharp whistle.

McFadden came around the corner of the building. "Yeah, Boss?"

"Get Birdie and comb this area for anything unusual. We have a scrap of cloth torn from what looks to be work pants or something similar. It's caught on the corner there. Get photos of everything, the ground, shrubs. Then bag it." He studied the area a moment. "Probably won't find anything useful since the place has been crawling with tourists all day."

"We had a good number of kids through today. They tend to ramble everywhere." Hannah picked up the cat and kissed his ear. "Good kitty."

Scoop eyed him then shook his head. In return, the cat gave him the stink-eye before turning his face up to Hannah and closing his eyes as she scratched under his chin.

* * *

After a preliminary check of the grounds around the entirety of the building and the collection of the bit of fabric from the scene, Hannah led Scoop along the driveway that passed in front of the Little White House. They walked around to the back of the structure, slipped under the privacy chain, and mounted the curving stairs to the main floor sun deck that overlooked a guard shack below and the descent down the mountain beyond.

The view at this time of day was spectacular. Scoop glanced down at her as she cleared her throat. "It'll be dark soon. I don't know…"

His hand on her arm stilled her words as he pointed toward the rear guard's shack just below them. A sandy-headed man in faded Army fatigues stood there with the cat at his side. They were both looking out over the steep wooded ravine as the sun eased behind the tip of the far mountain, bathing the area with the smoky violet hues of early twilight.

Scoop gestured for her to stay put as he quietly crossed the balcony to the staircase that led back down to the ground. As he stepped over the privacy chain, the man and cat turned and watched him.

"Who're you?" Scoop asked as he stopped a few feet from the rather unkempt stranger.

"Daxter. Folks call me Dax."

"In case you hadn't noticed, the museum closed a good while ago."

"Did it?"

"The lack of people and the fading light didn't give you a clue?"

"Guess I was caught up with the view."

"And I don't suppose you noticed all the police and the ambulance?"

"Somebody get hurt?"

"You could say that."

"One of those kids?"

"What do you know about the kids?"

"Only that they were bound to get into trouble." Dax shifted the backpack on his shoulders. "I went down by the little bridge over the creek to read in peace. Guess the time got away from me."

The cat stood and stretched, his hindquarters in the air, his toes spread. Then he gave himself a good shake. Scoop motioned with a lift of his chin. "That cat belong to you?"

"Callahan?" Dax looked down at the gray cat who had turned golden eyes on him. "No. He's his own cat as far as I know."

Hannah made her way down the stairs and stood beside Scoop. "I've seen you in town before."

Dax nodded. "I've been helping out in the kitchen at the Bulloch House for a few days. Bussing tables, washing dishes."

Scoop took a small step forward so that he partially shielded Hannah. "What made you decide to visit the museum today?"

"Came all this way to see it so I thought I'd better give it a look before I hit the road."

"Where you headed?"

Dax shrugged. "Anywhere. Nowhere. Got no agenda."

"A drifter, then."

"I prefer the term hobo."

"Drifter or hobo, I need to get a statement from you."

"A statement? About what?"

"About what you're doing at the museum."

"I just told you."

"Well, you can tell me again. For the record."

Chapter Four

Well, well. The Lawman is certainly a cool hand. That was one smooth interrogation. But my newfound friend took it in stride. I might add that the unexpected invitation to explain his presence at the museum only caused a momentary hesitation on his part. From the several cups of tea and the number of cookies he's consumed during the process, you'd think he had an ulterior motive in being so accommodating. I've been known to be agreeable to human interaction when the enticement is something good to eat. Or a cozy fire on a cold night.

Scoop drops Benjamin Matthew Daxter's expired driver's license on the break room table. "So, you just travel around the country? On foot?"

"My license is expired. And I don't own a car, so yeah. I travel mostly by hiking. Occasionally I hop a bus."

"Why?"

Dax's brow furrows slightly and he shrugs. "Why not? As good a way to see the country as any. Better, actually. You get to really see it."

"This address," *Scoop picks up the driver's license,* "in Nebraska. This was your last permanent address?"

"My mother still lives there."

"When were you last there?"

Dax's brow furrows deeper. "It's been a while."

"Define a while."

"Six years."

"And you've been bumming around from state to state all that time?"

Dax took a sip of the hot tea and replaced the cup on the saucer before answering. "I spent a little time out of the country."

"Where?"

"Afghanistan, mostly."

"Military?"

"Army."

That explains a lot, especially the fatigues and the sturdy boots. No shackles. Capable. And a free spirit. We're a bit alike, me and Benjamin Matthew Daxter. Both content with what comes our way. Yeah, I knew I liked this guy for some reason.

"So, after the lunch crowd, you walked along 27 to the museum?" *Scoop leans back in his chair, the notepad on the table in front of him untouched. I'm impressed at his lack of need to make notes.*

"Yep." *Dax eyes the nearly empty plate of cookies and his gaze drifts to me. He breaks one of the cookies and places it on a napkin on the floor by his chair.*

Lemon. With a creamy filling. Not bad. Not bad at all.

"Can you be more specific about the time?"

"Nope. I don't have a watch. I washed the last of the dishes. Decided I'd probably be on my way tomorrow so I headed toward the museum."

"Walk me through your time on the grounds."

Dax watches me a moment longer then looks Scoop in the eye with a sigh. "Traffic was light along the roadway. I turned off the highway onto Little White House Road. The shade was nice. At the ticket office I showed my military ID and got my ticket. Listened to the video presentation then took my time looking at all the exhibits." *He reaches down and scratches me behind my ears.* "I came through the shop to see FDR's unfinished portrait then out onto the grounds. I rambled around seeing the Avenue of the States' Stones, along the path to the Mustian house. The President's residence I saved for last."

"Any particular reason?"

"It's the big thing, isn't it? The place where our most beloved president felt at peace?"

"Then?"

"I came up the little rise to sit on the steps leading up to the guest quarters and the servants' quarters. Thought I'd sit in the sun and read a bit. That's when the group of little boys arrived, playing at being spies or assassins."

"And you decided to move along."

Dax nods.

"Move on to where?"

"The lane that passes in front of the Little White House has a trail off it that ends where they have some maintenance buildings. Another trail off to the left takes you to a small stream with a wooden foot bridge over it. A nice spot so I sat by a tree, got comfortable, and read a bit. I might have dozed for a while."

"Anyone see you?"

"I couldn't say. I did hear the sound of lawn equipment briefly but I didn't see it or the operator."

Scoop closes the notebook and taps it against the table. "You didn't think it was odd that a man was lying on the bed in the servants' quarters?"

"I didn't know there was a body in the servants' quarters. I didn't go up there."

"Why? It and the guest house are a major part of the museum."

Dax shrugs. "I don't know. I just didn't. I probably would have if the kids hadn't shown up and decided to make it the center of their battlefield."

"And you still say you don't know the victim other than having seen him around town."

"I still say it because it's still the truth. He ate at the Bulloch House a couple of times that I know of. I saw him on the main street. That's it."

Scoop stares at Dax with an unwavering eye. Finally, he stands and places the notebook in his jacket pocket. "I suggest you postpone your departure, Mr. Daxter, until this matter is cleared up."

The detective isn't satisfied with Dax's explanation. I don't blame him. If he knew what I saw, my new friend would be on his way to the pokey.

* * *

Scoop stood on the wide apron of the entrance to the museum and watched as the ex-army vet made his way at a leisurely pace along the drive in the deepening gloom. There was something there, he could feel it in his bones.

He took out his cell phone and tapped the surface a few

times, safely storing the interview with Benjamin Matthew Daxter in the cloud. Next, he punched in a phone number. When his brother answered, he told him what he needed.

When he hung up, he went back into the museum. He could see Hannah through the open doorway of her office. He turned left and went into the small theater. The video started up as he sat on one of the benches. It gave, in broad strokes, the story of FDR.

Scoop knew most of it, as did pretty much every native Georgian who had made their way through the school system. FDR was a big deal in the state of Georgia, even these many years after his service to the country and his untimely death.

Next, he walked slowly through the exhibit, viewing the life of the thirty-second president in the memorabilia of touring car, walking canes, eye-glasses, photographs, and, of course, the details of his involvement in the fight against polio.

Why had the killer chosen this public, revered place to display his victim?

* * *

Hannah was waiting just outside her office door when Scoop came out of the exhibit. "Can I let the staff go?"

"I should interview Shirley and then head on over to the hotel. The museum will have to remain closed tomorrow."

"Clay already determined that so we posted a bulletin on the park service website and sent out emails to the advanced ticket sales who gave us contact information. We'll have to post someone to turn away anyone else at the entrance."

"Good. Hopefully, we'll be able to clear this up quickly.

I'll need a list of everyone who works on the grounds, delivery people, dog walkers, anyone who has access to the site."

"There are no real barriers to access. Anyone could walk through the woods from the highway. The grounds keepers have some access trails as well. I'm sure some of the locals are aware of them but you don't think it could be someone from Warm Springs, do you?"

"Do you believe anyone outside the area would know how to get a body into the enclosed room?"

Hannah looked away. The thought that someone who lived in the area, someone that she most likely knew, could do such a thing was hard for her to accept. This was Warm Springs, Georgia, for goodness sake. There were no murderers here.

Her thoughts turned to Teagan and how the discovery of a dead body was going to impact her. She needed to collect her child and go home. The police and the state park law enforcement division could do their jobs but she'd had enough for one day. She needed to get Teagan away from all this talk of death and murder.

"If you don't mind, I think I'll take my daughter home. It's been an unsettling day."

Jackie was there with Teagan in Hannah's office, playing a card game. "Phyllis went back to the Lodge," she said. "We thought it would be best to have one less person underfoot. And Sue should have arrived there by now. We didn't want her wondering what happened to everyone."

"Good." Hannah ran her hand along Teagan's blond tresses. "Good. You should get on back as well. Teagan and I will drop you off."

Teagan looked from her mother to Scoop and back,

an anxious expression on her face. "But what about my statement? They need my statement, Mom."

"Clay already took your statement, sweetie."

"But I found the body." There was a note of pleading in her voice.

Scoop pulled a chair over to the desk and sat down. "Why don't we get this out of the way, huh? I like to get my facts firsthand anyway." He looked up at Hannah. "It won't take but a few minutes. If that's okay with you?"

Hannah was torn. Did she really want Teagan to rehash the events of the afternoon? Would she have nightmares about the dead body?

Scoop cleared his throat. "I find that it helps sometimes to talk things through, get any concerns out in the open and squared away. Kind of a release valve, you know?"

Teagan looked at her with pleading in those big blue eyes. "I can help, Mom. Honest."

"I really don't know what's best." Hannah knelt beside Tegan's chair. "I worry about you dwelling on what happened."

"But it's a mystery, Mom. Just like Nancy Drew. I've read all her books. I can help solve the case."

Scoop leaned in conspiratorially. "That's impressive. All of them?"

Teagan nodded. "And Harriet the Spy."

Hannah sighed and stood. "Well, keep it short, please. And then we're going to the Lodge and say hello to Sue before going straight home. Agreed?"

Teagan nodded then focused her attention on Scoop, her expression one of great seriousness.

"So," Scoop said, "walk me through what happened."

She thought for a moment. "They came back. After

Mom said they couldn't go up to the apartment they ran off, but then they came back."

"The boys who discovered the body?"

She nodded. "They started yelling so Fergus and I went to see what was wrong."

"Was anyone else around the building?"

She thought about it and nodded. "Earlier, some people came to the White House and went through the tour and back out but they didn't come up to the servants' quarters. They went on around the inner circle." Teagan settled more comfortably in the chair. "There was a man. He was with That Darn Cat."

"Teagan!" Hannah said

She looked up at her mother. "Well, that's what everyone calls him."

Scoop suppressed a smile. "His name is Callahan."

"Really?" Teagan's brow furrowed. "How do you know?"

"I'm a detective."

That seemed to satisfy her. "Anyway, there was a man and the cat. Callahan. The man was reading a book."

"What did you see when you went up the stairs?"

"One of the boys ran down and was headed toward the museum to tell. Then two more came down. When I got to the top of the stairs only one was there. He was angry."

"Why was he angry?"

"Because he thought a man was sleeping in the bed."

"And you didn't think he was asleep?"

She was quiet a moment, that contemplative look on her face. "No. He didn't move and the way he was laying wasn't like someone asleep."

"How do you mean?"

"It was awkward. You know? When you get ready to go to sleep you get in a comfortable position."

"That's very good, Teagan." Scoop looked up at Hannah. "Did anyone move the body?"

"No one on the museum staff. Oscar and I went in when he and Harry opened the Plexiglas." She turned her gaze to the window of her office. "I knew he was dead before I touched him."

"Where did you touch him?"

"I checked his throat for a pulse."

"Anywhere else?"

She shook her head.

"And Oscar?"

"No."

Scoop sat back in his chair, his arms crossed over his chest, a distant look on his face. After a moment he came out of his reverie. "Did anything else strike you as odd, Teagan? Other than the way he was lying?"

"There was a mark on the floor right at the door. Black like my boots make on the car door when I push it open with my foot. The door cut right across it."

Scoop grinned. "You're a good detective, Teagan, with an excellent eye for detail."

She smiled.

Chapter Five

Well, this is certainly working out in my favor. The little girl, Teagan, is proving to be quite the detective-in-training. She was able to communicate to Cool Hand Luke that most important bit of information about the drag marks on the threshold of the apartment. It's a helpful fact but I had already decided that the victim had been killed somewhere else. The question is where?

Scoop seems to be far away with his thoughts as we watch Hannah, Teagan, and Jackie drive away from the museum. Now all I have to do is contrive to tag along with him so I can get to the hotel and determine the facts first hand.

He's looking down at me, having become aware of my presence. It's time he learned what's what or I'll have to waste a lot of precious time convincing him to follow my lead. There is always that one human in the bunch that refuses to see the wisdom of what's before his eyes. If there's one thing I hate, it's herding humans. Which is quite a different thing from bending them to my will.

I wonder what Lil the Librarian had for tea?

Enough of that! This isn't the time to let my preoccupation with food distract me.

I trail after Scoop as he heads back inside the museum in search of Clay. He's huddled up with Shirley, the shop attendant, ticket taker, and woman of many talents. I say a woman of many talents because as I speak, with thoughts of Lil and her delicious teas still spinning in my head, Shirley plunks a large dollop of homemade banana pudding on a container lid and places it on the floor for me. I think I'm in love.

I keep my ear to the conversation even as I indulge in a mouth-watering sweet treat covered in meringue. I doubt even the Lodge at Callaway could produce such a feast to the old taste buds.

"This Frenchie name the victim had, could you be more specific?" *Scoop asks.*

"Like I told Clay, it was something like I remember from history class. You know, DeSoto or d'Iberville or something like that. With a de at the beginning."

So, someone with a French or Spanish name. Got it. Surely the hotel will know.

"Remember a first name?"

Shirley shakes her head. "Honestly, he probably said but it didn't stick. And that was two, three days ago. I get so many folks through the shop. They all want to talk about FDR, especially the older ones, tell about their parents or grandparents who were around during his presidency. And they talk about themselves, too. So, I automatically filter out most of it. Not that I'm not interested. I enjoy a good jaw wag with folks but my old brain can't hang on to all of it. His last name stood out because it was foreign sounding."

"And you're sure it was the man in the servants' quarters?"

"I'm sure."

"Did you go into the apartment?"

"No. Clay showed me a photo on his phone."

Scoop stares pensively out the window then nods. "Nothing else you remember about him? Any of his conversation?"

"He was asking about the President's life before he got elected. Looking for anything about that particularly."

"And?"

"I showed him the books we have that give an overview of his life. That didn't interest him much. He really seemed to want to pick my brain about him. 'Course I know all about him. The whole town knows. But it was like the President's time on the mountain didn't interest him. Odd, really."

"Nothing else?"

"'Fraid not," *Shirley says as she hands Scoop a collection of pamphlets about the museum and the grounds. Just as he's about to turn away, she holds up her finger.* "There was one odd thing."

"Yeah?"

She now has my full attention and Scoop's.

"There was another guy in here at the time. He ambled around looking at stuff. Wore a cap pulled low and kept his head down." *She gives a knowing nod.* "Suspicious like. Thought he might be a shoplifter so I watched him close."

"And?" *Scoop places the brochures on the counter and takes out his notebook.*

"Didn't buy anything, of course. Hung about the exit door to the exhibition room a couple of minutes after the Frenchie left, then followed after."

Well, well, this is interesting. It seems our victim was being tailed by someone. The killer, perhaps?

"You didn't recognize this man?"

"No. As I said, he kept a baseball cap pulled low over his face. Had longish hair. It curled along the back of his neck, over his ears, and the sides of his face."

"So, you don't know if he was local?"

Shirley shakes her head. So much for that hot tip. Of course, the resolution of this case isn't going to be as simple as that but a cat can always hope.

"Tell me what you remember about him."

"The cap had the Atlanta Braves logo on it but then you see those everywhere around here. He was shorter than the Frenchie. Probably about five-eight to five-ten, something like that. And he had a tattoo. It was on his left arm. You could only see part of it where the shirt sleeve ended on his upper arm."

Shirley closes her eyes as she concentrates. Scoop waits patiently without speaking or fidgeting. A solid quality in a detective, if you ask me.

"Military, I think." *Shirley opens her eyes and smiles.* "The bottom portion was part of a globe with a bit of banner running across it that wasn't visible because of the sleeve. Of course, these days a lot of people who have nothing to do with the military get similar tattoos."

And just as quickly as Shirley gives us hope, she pops our bubble with an incontrovertible fact of today's fashion trend.

Scoop replaces his notebook in his inner coat pocket along with the brochures Shirley gave him. I think we are done here. For the moment.

Where next, I wonder. My guess would be the B&B. McFadden and Birdie left to set up an incident room at the local police station some twenty minutes ago. Hannah balked at the idea of using the video room at the museum. Scoop's reassurance that they would only need it for a couple of days failed to sway her.

Clay supported her stance. Even a newbie in the romance department can guess motivation. There was the hint of the territorial male in his attitude toward Scoop. And rightly so. Disinterested as I am in the courting ways of humans, I can see that there's something there between Scoop and Hannah.

The police station isn't that far away but I don't have the luxury of a car at my disposal. And while I'm quite capable of getting where I need to be, time is another matter. This complicates things for me. Smart as I am, it's difficult to be in the know of what's happening on the case when all the critical areas of interest are spread out all over the place. Challenge accepted. I've never failed in my ability to bend the human will to my wants and needs. Well, mostly never. Okay, it's a fifty-fifty proposition but I'm up to it.

Scoop is proving to be quite a pain, though he's quick on the uptake. He's willing to act when he sees what's plainly in front of him. He's preparing to leave the museum so I'll have to convince him that he needs my help. That it's essential, really. I may not have his credentials, but I am a very clever cat.

Tricky. He's not one to give much away. Yes, a real Cool Hand Luke. If I'm going to tag along, I'll have to forget my dignity though it pains me to do so. Curiosity. It will be the death of me. Or at least my pride.

I hurry along after him as he heads for his car. Deception won't work with him. He's much too sharp to fall for my usual tricks. I'll just have to sit on the curb as he climbs into the car and beg. I give a pitiful cry. How degrading.

He looks down at me, the car door still open, as he weighs his options. A glance up the steps to the entrance of the museum seems to convince him.

"Well, come on if you're coming," *he says.*

I leap onto his lap and over to the passenger seat, well pleased with myself. Maybe Cool Hand Luke is more malleable than I originally thought.

He starts the car but sits with the motor idling as he punches the screen of his phone with a forefinger. Birdie's voice fills the car. I look around but there's no sign of her. Kind of creepy, if you ask me. Could this be the ESP that Lil is always talking about?

"Yeah, Birdie," *Scoop says,* "you have an address for the museum's assistant director?"

"I can get it. I'm still at the police station. Why?"

"The cat." *Scoop eyes me.* "He got left behind at the museum."

"I don't think he belongs to her. I don't think he belongs to anyone."

Scoop is silent for a moment. He scowls. "Just text me her address." *He stabs the phone with his finger and Birdie's voice disappears in mid-sentence. Scoop has a scowl on his face.*

Well, well, what have we here?

* * *

Scoop was irritated with himself. He liked to keep his cards close to his vest. Now Birdie would have a bee in her bonnet. He had heard it in her tone of voice. He should have just left That Darn Cat to fend for himself. A far more fitting name, he decided, than Callahan. But, if he was being honest with himself, he had wanted the excuse to see Hannah away from the crime scene. Why? Because he had steered clear of Hannah Wilson when she was a freshman at college because of her brother, Eddie. You don't mess with the team dynamic. No matter how attractive the enticement. The success of the team was his success and he had been on his way to The Show.

Still, Eagle Eye Eddie's little sister had been something. It was odd that he had been so attracted to her back then. She hadn't been his type. Too shy and quiet. He had liked a goodtime girl back then. A girl like Rita. He smiled at the thought. He wouldn't mind a good dose of Rita right now.

The smile faded. Rita, the goodtime girl, had disappeared with the good times. A career-ending injury had ended their relationship almost as quickly as his name had faded from the headlines of the sports section of the paper.

Scoop gave a bark of laughter as he shifted the car into gear and headed toward Hwy 27. What in the devil was wrong with him? He shook his head as he turned toward the heart of Warm Springs. The cat had given him a startled look then placed his front paws on the dashboard and stared out the windshield as if he was anticipating their next move.

Their next move? Scoop laughed again at the idiocy of his thoughts. As if the cat could somehow help solve the crime. The sight of Hannah had obviously affected him more than he realized. He was acting like a character out of *Alice in Wonderland.* Well, why not?

The little town of Warm Springs had that lost-in-time feel that brought to mind the simpler days of the past when Franklin Delano Roosevelt came to enjoy the healing qualities of the springs and start a nationwide crusade against polio. Twilight was deepening toward evening, and the lights of the quaint shops on either side of Broad Street created a warm glow. Scoop pulled into a parking slot in front of the Hotel Warm Springs.

As he got out of the car, the cat leaped over the console

and quickly out the door. Scoop hadn't counted on this turn of events and wasn't sure what to do. May in Georgia is almost as hot as July and August. Even though the sun had set, it was still much too hot to leave the cat in the car. But what to do with him? Nothing, he decided. They were on the cat's turf.

All of these thoughts ran through Scoop's mind as he watched the cat sit on the sidewalk and look up at him. Expectantly.

"Hmm," Scoop said. He hit the lock button on the key fob. "Let me guess. You're going to let me be the point man this time."

The cat flicked his right ear and gave Scoop a look that suggested his patience was wearing thin. Or that Scoop was a little slow on the uptake.

The roadbed through the little town was cut deep so all the shops were built above street level. Several steps led from the curb up to the sidewalk. Scoop mounted the steps and turned to survey the heart of Warm Springs. The row of businesses on either side of the street were picturesque, having been built in a bygone era. He doubted it had changed much in the years since the thirty-second president put the place on the map with his decision to build a retreat there.

The tail end of the row across from him was occupied by a two story, white, clapboard building reminiscent of a stately home. It housed The Bulloch House Restaurant. At least they wouldn't starve over the course of the investigation. He'd need to interview the staff to nail down the particulars of Daxter's statement.

A trickle of people strolled the sidewalks, some going to or from the restaurant. Others merely window shopped.

Scoop noticed that people spoke in passing, occasionally pausing to chat. An elderly couple with a dog sat on a bench in the front of the mercantile shop across the way, eating ice cream cones. Warm Springs definitely moved at a slower pace.

The three story, painted brick building of the B&B was old. It anchored the end of the row of businesses with a parking lot at the side. The far side of the parking lot gave way to railway tracks.

The lobby was interesting. Dark stained wood of the reception desk and staircase was the dominant feature, lightened by the tile floor and painted wood paneling. Framed newspaper articles, photographs, and memorabilia of FDR and his famous guests served as the décor. At the foot of the stairs sat an ancient wheelchair. Scoop wondered if it was one that FDR had actually used.

A gentle *tink, tink* sounded from above stairs. The reception desk was unmanned. Scoop studied some of the framed articles about FDR and Warm Springs. He went through the doorway to the adjacent Tuscawilla Soda Shop. It, too, was unmanned.

The cat took an inordinate interest in the menu board. Scoop had to admit the place smelled delicious in a sweet, sugary way. It was enough to tempt anyone.

He went back into reception, the cat trailing his footsteps, and up the stairs. The second-floor landing held a sitting room at the front of the building and a hallway leading toward the back with rooms opening on either side. Footsteps from above led him to the third floor. There, the stairway opened into a dining area with a view out onto the main street. He discovered the source of the sound. A woman was setting up the dining table with utensils and china.

"Good evening," he said.

She looked up from her task and smiled. "Hello." She turned the last coffee cup upside down in the saucer and approached him with a smile. "You must be the detective from Atlanta."

"Scoop Russell." He shook the offered hand. "The rest of the team will be along shortly."

"A bit of excitement, isn't it, here in sleepy little Warm Springs? Nothing like this has happened since the shoot-out between Bulloch and Thompson in this very room."

"Oh?"

She gave a dismissive wave of her hand. "Long before my time. You should talk to the owner. She's owned the hotel some thirty odd years. And no relation, by the way, to the original owner. The grand feud between Bulloch and Thompson is just part of the hotel's history."

"So, you know why we're here."

"Of course. Everyone does, I expect. Small towns and their gossip, you know. Not much happens that we aren't aware of." She leaned in slightly. "Who is it?"

"Pardon?"

"The body. Who is it?" She did a little meh movement with her head. "Billy Brad wouldn't say."

Good for Billy Brad, Scoop thought. "We don't have a positive I.D. yet. No one at the museum knew his name."

The woman considered this. "But someone did recognize him, didn't they?"

"Do you have a full house right now, Ms.—I'm sorry, I didn't catch your name?"

"I'm Alice. The owner is away at the moment so I guess you could say I'm in charge. And, no, we don't. I've let the three rooms for you and your associates. I'm putting you in 112, by the way. It has a view of Broad Street and the intersection. Three other rooms are currently occupied." She paused. "Well, they were. One of the guests checked out early this morning."

"Who was that guest, if I may ask?"

She watched his face. "Is that an official inquiry?"

"Curiosity, let's say."

Alice glanced beyond him and frowned. "That Darn Cat."

The gray cat sat on the landing near the top of the stairs. At Alice's words, he turned his head in a nonchalant manner as if he were examining the woodwork of the ceiling.

Scoop gave a slight shake of his head. "He's taken up with me for some reason."

"I can't have a cat wandering the place. I have to think about the other guests."

"I imagine he'll wander off when he gets bored." Scoop cleared his throat. "Now about that early departure?"

"A woman. Name of Joyce Favor."

"Had she been here long?"

"Almost a week. She had the room reserved through the weekend but said something had come up at home that required her attention."

"Did she happen to mention where home was?"

"No. But she wasn't southern."

"Did she have an accent?"

"Yes," Alice smiled and her eyes twinkled. "Posh."

"I see."

"I don't think you do." Alice gestured toward the stairs. "Shall we get you registered?"

"Sure." Scoop fell in step behind Alice and the cat followed on his heels. "Anything else you can tell me about her?"

"Attractive. Very. Dark hair, medium length. Blue eyes. Slender and tall." She went behind the registration desk. "Soft spoken and kind."

"Kind?"

"Always a thank you for any little attention, or holding the door for someone to come or go. Bought Tracey's little girl an ice cream. That kind of thoughtfulness."

She turned the old-fashioned registry book toward Scoop for him to sign. "The room's unlocked." She took a key from one of the pigeon holes mounted on the wall behind the desk. "I don't have a safe in the room but if there's anything of value you're concerned about, I can lock it up for you here at the desk."

"Good to know." He signed where she indicated and let his gaze travel up the page, making a mental note of the names. "Tell me about your other guests."

"Not much to tell. And I respect our guests' privacy."

"Alvin Williams. Checked in three days ago. What does he look like?"

Alice didn't answer immediately. Finally, she asked, "Do you think he's the dead man?"

"Why do you ask that?"

"He hasn't slept in his bed for the last two nights. He wasn't at breakfast yesterday or this morning."

"Huh," Scoop took his notebook from the inner pocket of his coat. "Did he say why he was in Warm Springs?"

"Business. Said he had been on the road for several weeks and just needed a couple of days' break. Thought exploring the area with the hiking and such would set him up for the rest of his road trip."

"Old? Young? Short? Tall?"

"Middle aged. Average height. A little heavy around the middle but that goes with being a traveling salesman, I suppose. But fit otherwise."

"Hair? Eyes?"

"Brunette. A lot of it and needing a haircut. But clean shaven. Can't say for sure about the eye color."

"Did he express an interest in the museum? Is that why he stopped over in Warm Springs?"

"Not really. He read some of the articles," she indicated the various framed pieces concerning FDR with a jerk of her head, "but seemed more interested in the mountain."

"Thanks." Scoop glanced down at the registry. "What about Curtis Arthur D'Amboise? That's quite a flourish to his signature. He's been here for some time. What's his story?"

"Journalist. He's researching the Roosevelts for a book, he says. Wanted to know all the local stories."

"You don't sound as though you liked him."

"I don't like or dislike him. Strikes me as a kind of fancy man."

"Fancy man?"

"You know the type. Nice looking and knows it. Charming when it serves the situation. Uses both, I suspect, for no good purpose."

"You have a very discerning eye, Alice."

"The hotel business brings you in contact with all types. After a while you begin to pick up on the little things."

"Anything in particular about Mr. D'Amboise that put you off?"

"He was taken with Ms. Favor. Tried to chat her up but she wasn't having it. Asked me about her, who she was and why she was in Warm Springs."

"Why was she in Warm Springs?"

"Vacation, she said."

"But?"

Alice shrugged. "But nothing."

"Other than nice looking, what did Mr. D'Amboise look like?"

"Tall, slim. Very white teeth."

The cat jumped from the floor to the registry desk and put his nose to the open page of the registry book. He appeared to be sniffing down the page. Then he put both front paws against Scoop's chest.

Scoop ran his hand along the cat's back. Curtis Arthur D'Amboise. A Frenchie name if there ever was one.

* * *

Hannah, Jackie, Phyllis, Sue, and Teagan sat at one of the al fresco tables on the fringe of the courtyard of Carson's Tap Room at the Calloway Garden's Lodge. Fergus sat quietly at Teagan's feet, well out of the way of foot traffic. Hannah had ordered a glass of wine to be sociable with her sorority sisters but she had barely tasted it. The drive home along the twisting roads of Pine Mountain after the stressful day she'd had caused her to refrain from imbibing more than a few sips.

In truth, the events of the day put a real damper on what had been meant to be a fun reunion with her dear friends. Their days together at college had been the best time of Hannah's life. They had nurtured each other through trials, tribulations, love, heartache, joy, and achievement. Now, a murder at the museum had destroyed any hope of the occasion being the happy celebration it was meant to be.

She was concerned about the effects of the day's events on Teagan and hoped the semblance of normalcy with "The Girls" would distract her from all that had happened. During the drive over Teagan had been quiet, eyes forward but Hannah knew that look of concentration. She had also been keenly aware of the fact that Teagan had placed Fergus in the knee space of the front seat and kept kneading his fur with her hand.

For his part, Fergus leaned into Teagan's legs, his head on her knees, never taking his eyes off her. It had been a good move to adopt him after David's death. She was thankful to Sue for suggesting it. Teagan had slowly come out of her shell over the past two years. The connection between her and the Scottie had given her focus and a sense of security. Hannah was concerned that this murder would cause her to retreat into her own private world again.

The conversation had been noticeably steered toward the three friends, their family lives, and humorous episodes of the past when the four of them roomed together. The remnants of their light meal of sandwiches and salads were strewn about the table and the forced gaiety was petering out. Hannah pulled her wallet from her purse.

"It's getting late and I need to get Teagan home." She glanced at her bill and counted out cash to cover it. "Let's touch base mid-morning tomorrow, shall we? We can set our agenda then."

"Mid-morning suits me." Jackie glanced down her bill and took a credit card from her purse. "I have a massage scheduled for nine."

"And I'm sleeping in," Phyllis said. She yawned. "It's been a busy two weeks at the office, trying to clear my calendar for this break, and I'm pooped. I'm glad we'll have four days at the Lodge in reasonable quiet before things start heating up for the Memorial Day weekend next week."

Sue reached down and scratched Fergus behind the ears. "You're such a good dog. So quiet and polite." She smiled at Teagan. "You've taken good care of him."

Teagan offered up a hint of a smile but made no reply.

"Off we go, then," said Hannah.

The girls blew air kisses all around and departed to their different destinations.

It was a dark night and Hannah was glad she'd been temperate with the wine. The drive seemed to take longer in the darkness and as they pulled into the driveway at their home, Hannah felt a shiver run down her spine.

Weeks earlier, the sensor for the flood lights on the carport had gone on the fritz. Now, all that welcomed them was a weak beacon from the light over the back door. The events of the day did nothing to dispel the sense of eeriness at the prospect of entering a dark house. Hannah opted for a cheery note as she opened the car door.

"Come along, you two. It's past my bedtime and I can't wait for a good hot bath."

The moment Fergus bounded out of the car, he took a rigid stance. He gave a low woof.

"Fergus," Hannah said, "come along. It's late and we want our beds."

Fergus took a couple of cautious steps toward the back door and stopped again. He gave another woof then a deep throated growl.

Hannah put out her hand to keep Teagan behind her. "What is it, old boy?"

He sniffed along the pathway then up the steps to the back door. Hannah followed after, her key fob in her hand, her thumb on the alarm button. The nearest house belonged to the Sedgwicks and was a quarter of a mile away, their outdoor pole fixture a distant halo of light against the night sky.

Fergus woofed again as he stood with his nose to the door. To Hannah's surprise, it wasn't completely closed. The tongue of the door lock had not engaged. She pushed on the door and it swung open. Fergus dashed into the room, his toenails making a skittering sound against the linoleum of the old kitchen floor.

Hannah felt her heart thumping in her chest. She reached through the opening and flipped the switch. The kitchen sprang into high relief with the flood of light from the overhead fixture. There was no one there.

The Scottie raced down the hallway, running from room to room. Hannah followed in his wake, flipping switches until there was no dark corner in the house. She checked the front door and found it securely locked.

In the kitchen, she found Teagan standing in the middle of the room, her face pale. Hannah felt her heart jump in her chest at the stricken look on her daughter's face. She smiled and gave a deep, exaggerated sigh. "Silly, Fergus," she said, "chasing his tail." She dropped her keys on the kitchen table. "And silly me for leaving the door unlocked this morning. What was I thinking?" She pulled Teagan close in a bear hug. How could she have forgotten to lock the door?

"I'll have to get my head out of the clouds and be more mindful, won't I?" She held Teagan at arms' length. "Cocoa, don't you think? Just the thing we need to get a good night's sleep."

Fergus had returned to the kitchen. He kept going to the door and circling back to Teagan as if he were herding her. She crouched beside him and scratched behind his ears. "It's okay," she said. "There's no one here but us."

Chapter Six

I stare into Scoop's eyes, willing him to understand. He gives me a scratch under the chin then promptly lifts me by my mid-section and places me on the floor.

Stubborn mule!

He proceeds to show the hotel manager an image on his phone. I can only assume by the way she recoils that it's a photo of the dead man in the servants' quarters.

"Is this Curtis Arthur D'Amboise?" *Scoop asks.*

Alice nods. "How did he die?"

"We don't have the coroner's report yet. Do you know where Mr. D'Amboise lived?"

"Florida. Somewhere in Florida. He said where but I can't think at the moment."

Florida? Why would a journalist from Florida be keen on a book about FDR? I can only imagine that anyone who would take on the task of writing something about Roosevelt would have a particular interest in him. The life of the thirty-second president is certainly well known. Anyone who hangs out at the Tourist Information Center just across the railroad tracks can tell you that. Trudy is a walking encyclopedia about the man. Whatever an encyclopedia is. She also makes delicious deviled eggs. But that's beside the point.

Roosevelt is probably the most written about president after George Washington. Well, there is that guy Kennedy, I suppose. Trudy holds him in almost the same esteem as Roosevelt. The question is, what inspired this interest on the part of Curtis Arthur D'Amboise?

"I need to see his room, please." Scoop returns the phone to his pocket.

Alice takes a key from the cubby hole behind the desk. "This way."

We follow her up the stairs to the second floor and along the hallway toward the back of the hotel. She unlocks the door.

Scoop takes the key from her. "If you'd wait in the hallway, please."

He makes no effort to block me, thankfully.

All the elements of the hotel reflect the era in which it was built. The room contains an iron bedstead and valanced drapes. In the corner is mounted a sink which, I'm sure, was a convenience in the days before the notion of the individual bath. It would be just the thing for a movie setting.

Scoop stands inside the doorway, hands in his pockets and surveys the room. I've come to realize that this is his process so I shall sit quietly until he's satisfied.

A suitcase sits on a chair, partially closed with clothes spilling out of it. I'm itching to get my paws on its contents.

But Scoop is in no hurry to start with the obvious. Instead, he crosses the room and looks out the window. I join him to see that there *is nothing to see.*

This side of the hotel overlooks the parking lot and, in the back corner of the property, a little gardening shed surrounded by plants, an arbor, and a swing. A nice little private spot to relax and eat an ice cream or rest one's weary paws after a day of sightseeing around Warm Springs and Pine Mountain. I've been known to take advantage of the spot on occasion.

Two cars are parked below. In the near distance is an intersection. On the corner is a gas station and beyond that is a Dollar General, the eyesore of modern commerce's sprawl toward the little business district.

Finally, Scoop turns to the desk. It's strewn about with papers, pamphlets, and a steno pad with odd scribblings.

I hop onto the chair to get a better look. It's all Greek to me, seeing as how I can't read. It's just a bunch of initials. Or perhaps, they're abbreviations. There are symbols as well. It's obvious that d'Amboise had his own version of shorthand. Was he being secretive or simply efficient?

Scoop pulls on a glove from his outer coat pocket and sifts through it all.

At last, he turns to the suitcase. Our man Curtis was messy. All of his clothing is tossed about as if … What's this! This case has been rifled or I'm not a curious cat. Scoop has cottoned on to the idea as well. He runs his gloved hand along the interior of the lid of the old leather suitcase. It has been ripped open. The musty scent of old cloth suggests the tearing is new.

We look at each other. Two like minds coming to the same deduction. Someone has been here before us.

* * *

Scoop considered the state of D'Amboise's possessions then stepped to the door. "Could you come into the room, please," he asked Alice.

"My word," she said.

"Was Mr. D'Amboise an untidy guest?"

"Not particularly. He had notes and a few books on the desk. Some brochures from the local attractions."

"So, you would say this wasn't typical of his room?"

"Certainly not."

"Can you say if anything's missing?"

Alice walked to the door of the adjoining bathroom and checked the medicine cabinet. Then she looked in the armoire. Finally, she scrutinized the desk.

"His laptop is missing. Sometimes there was a notebook as well."

"When was the last time you were in here?"

"Yesterday. Just before noon."

"And when did you last see Mr. D'Amboise?"

"Yesterday. In the afternoon. He said he needed to go into LaGrange and might not return until today."

"Did he tell you why?"

"No, only that he needed to check something and might need to stay the night."

"Can you be more specific about your last encounter? The time? Where?"

"It was gone three o'clock. He came into the Tuscawilla for an ice cream. I made fresh peach yesterday."

"We need to block off this room. No one in or out until my team has processed it."

"There are only three of us, with the owner out of town. Ida Mae helps with the cleaning. Molly works the ice cream shop and whatever else is needed when things get busy."

Scoop watched the cat as he poked his head under the mid-section of the bed then proceeded to crawl under it.

"Thank you, Alice. My team should be along in a few minutes. Please send them up here."

Alice hesitated then nodded. Scoop could sense her curiosity but he had no intention of allowing her to remain in the room and observe him following the lead of a cat. As she disappeared down the hallway, Scoop closed the door.

An Oriental carpet covered most of the floor. Scoop got down on his knees and lifted the bedding. The cat lay on his belly, facing the head of the bed where the rug ended.

Scoop used the light on his phone to illuminate the space. There was nothing to see. "Not such a super sleuth after all," he said to the cat.

Ears flattened, the cat turned to Scoop and gave him a look that said volumes.

Scoop chuckled and stood. He tapped his phone and dialed Birdie. While he waited for her to answer, he opened the drawers of the desk and poked around the contents.

"Yeah, Boss?" Birdie sounded a little out of breath.

"Where are you?"

"Just entering the hotel now."

"We've found our victim's identity. The manager will show you to his room." He paused. "Someone's been here before us."

"Dang."

Within a couple of minutes Birdie was standing in the doorway, case in hand. The cat stuck his head out from beneath the bed. Scoop decided it was time to rid himself of his presence. He'd take him to Hannah. Just to get him out of the middle of his investigation, he told himself.

He picked the cat up and turned to Birdie who was pulling on a pair of gloves. "You get that address for me?"

She gave him the side eye. "Know her from your college days, do ya?"

"Knew her brother. He was on the team. I wouldn't have recognized her except for the eyes. Just like her brother's."

"Uh huh."

"Don't start with that, Birdie."

Birdie gave him a wide-eyed look. "With what?"

Scoop sighed. "The address?"

Birdie took out her phone and shared the contact info to his. "She's very pretty."

"I noticed."

Birdie grinned. "I bet you did."

Scoop wasn't going to engage in Birdie's word game. He turned to the door. The cat squirmed free, leapt to the floor, and back under the bed.

"What the heck, Callahan?"

"Callahan?"

"That's what Daxter called him. I'm beginning to think it fits."

The cat stuck his head out from under the bed.

"I can see why he'd think that. McFadden will get a hoot out of that. Look at him. He's giving you the stare. Plus, he obviously prefers my company to yours. Very discerning taste, if you ask me."

"Ha, ha." Scoop sighed again. "He's a pain. What am I supposed to do with him? The hotel manager doesn't want him roaming the place and upsetting the other guests."

Birdie shrugged. "The little girl says he belongs to the town. I imagine the hotel manager is only making noise just in case any of us object to the cat roaming the place."

"Well, I do object. He doesn't need to be in the middle

of our crime scene."

"I doubt this is the scene of the crime."

"You know what I mean."

Birdie ducked her head as she gave a half smile. "Sure thing, boss. You might get the museum's assistant director to corral him while we're here. She seems to like animals."

Scoop felt his ears redden and was thankful Birdie was focused on photographing the scene. The fact that she had voiced exactly what he wanted to do irked him. Was he that transparent?

He looked at his watch. He had sixty-eight hours before he had to cancel his fishing trip for the Memorial Day weekend. It was time to focus on the job at hand.

He took out his phone and dialed Hannah Sanderson's number. When she answered she sounded distracted.

"Scoop Russell, Mrs. Sanderson. I wonder if you can help me out with a situation."

"Situation?"

"The cat."

"Oh. I'd forgotten all about him."

"He seems hell bent on mucking up my investigation."

"Right … well…"

Hannah was clearly distracted. In fact, Scoop thought he detected a hint of distress in her voice.

"I just got Teagan to bed and I'm getting out of the shower. I don't really know who to call to deal with him. I suppose Clay could have someone collect him from the museum."

"He's not at the museum. We're at the hotel."

"Oh. The Hotel Warm Springs? How did he get there?"

Scoop hesitated. "He's resourceful."

"I see."

Scoop doubted very much that she did. "He's contaminating my investigation. I don't have time to wrangle a curious cat."

"I'll speak with Alice. The hotel is pet friendly."

"But my crime scene isn't."

"Oh. Right." Hannah took a sharp breath. "Was he murdered at the hotel?"

Scoop silently cursed himself. "No. But the victim was staying here."

There was a brief silence from Hannah's end of the call. "I don't know what you expect me to do."

"Look," Scoop said, "I only have two more days to close this case. I can't afford to have the evidence contaminated. I'm bringing the cat to you."

With that, he hung up before she could voice an objection.

* * *

Hannah wiped the steam from the bathroom mirror. Her hair was wet, she had on no make-up, and those were definitely dark circles under her eyes. There was nothing she could do about any of it because Scoop Russell was less than ten minutes away. She ran a comb through her hair, threw the wet towel over the shower curtain rod, and dashed to her room to throw on a pair of jeans and an overly large tee shirt with the Atlanta Braves logo on the front.

Fergus came to the door of Teagan's room and watched her flying around the house stashing dirty cups in the dishwasher, throwing her walking shoes into the laundry room, and picking up various items of books, iPad, and mismatched socks and stuffing them wherever she could find a hidden spot.

He stood and watched her with a touch of anxiety in his body language. First, he would check on Teagan who had fallen into an exhausted sleep after her quick bath and a cup of hot chocolate, then he would take a couple of steps out of her room to monitor Hannah buzzing about the house.

Hannah stuffed the dirty pair of socks into a vase on the mantle and came to give him a comforting scratch behind the ear. The sound of a car's engine caused him to bristle.

"It's okay, Fergus. It's a friend not a foe." But, still, she lifted the café curtain over the back door window to see that it was indeed Scoop. He was trying to hold on to a very unhappy cat squirming in his arms as he approached.

She opened the door as he mounted the steps and quickly closed it behind him as he released Callahan. Fergus gave a soft woof from his stance in the hallway guarding Teagan's door. Callahan bowed his back and hissed in the dog's direction before sitting under the butcher block work station and proceeding to nonchalantly groom his paw.

One look at Scoop revealed who had really won the encounter.

"Your cat…" he began.

"He's not my cat."

"Well, whoever he belongs to, he's a problem."

She lightly touched the small scratch on the side of Scoop's jaw and quickly drew her hand back. "He did that?"

"Yes."

Scoop's hissed response was as pointed as Callahan's had been.

"It's hard to believe."

"Well, believe it." Scoop let go of his annoyance with a *mea culpa* grin. "But I don't think it was intentional. He simply didn't want to get in the car."

"Most cats don't like to ride."

"That's not it. He was in his element when we drove from the museum to the hotel."

"Huh. I guess he wanted to stay at the hotel."

"You think?"

Hannah felt the blush running up her neck and face.

Scoop was immediately contrite. "Sorry. Didn't mean to bark at you. I'm under pressure to get to the bottom of this case."

"Big Memorial Day plans?"

His grin turned sheepish. "Something like that."

"Well, I hope you get to the bottom of it quickly, too." She rubbed her upper arms as the memory of the opened back door flashed through her mind.

Scoop frowned. "Everything okay? You seem spooked."

The blush deepened. "I guess I am. After the events of the day, we arrived home to find that I'd failed to properly close and lock the door this morning." She shrugged.

"This door?" Scoop turned to the back door and checked the doorknob. It turned smoothly. He opened it a few inches then released it. The door swung smoothly closed with a decided click. "It was open or just unlocked?"

"Both."

"You're sure you forgot?"

Hannah hugged herself. "Not really. I never have before. We're pretty isolated here. You can barely see the Sedgwick's house at the top of the rise. And it's just me and Teagan."

Callahan had been watching them throughout this exchange and he moved to the door and began to sniff around. He soon gave up that pursuit and came to wind his way between Hannah's legs. She picked him up and held him to her chest as she softly scratched behind his ears.

"Have you called the local police?"

Hannah gave a little worried laugh. "Because I forgot to lock the back door? No, I'm not someone who cries wolf over my own forgetfulness."

Scoop stared at the door then at the way Hannah held the cat so close. "You should call them."

"I'd be too embarrassed."

He considered this a minute and looked down the hallway where Fergus was a rigid bundle of energy torn between the urge to be at Hannah's side and the need to guard Teagan's room. "Is the dog a good watchdog?"

Hannah turned and followed his gaze. "Fergus? He's excellent. In every way."

"Good." Scoop hesitated a moment. "Did you recognize the dead man? Curtis Arthur D'Amboise?"

"Is that his name?"

"Yes. He's been at the hotel for a couple of weeks."

She shook her head. "No." She frowned. "But I only took that one quick look when I checked his pulse." She hugged Callahan more tightly. "It was unnerving."

"I'm sure it was."

She kneaded the cat's fur. "It was so unreal."

Scoop took her elbow and turned her toward the front of the house. In the living room he directed her to the couch then sat in an armchair angled toward her. He took out his phone, hesitated, then asked, "Would you be up to looking at a photo of him to be sure?"

Hannah stared into Scoop's eyes. She didn't want to look at the photo. She wanted the long, horrible day to disappear into forgetfulness. She wanted life to return to normal, for Warm Springs to once again be the safe, familiar haven that sheltered her and her child. She nodded.

He flicked through the photos until he found the one he wanted and held the phone for her to see. She took it from his hand and studied the face of the dead man.

Finally, she shook her head. "I don't think so. I could have seen him in passing and it not register. With the warm spring weather, the museum has had a lot of traffic. I feel certain that I haven't had any interaction with him."

"He's been in town for over two weeks. The hotel manager tells me he's researching a book on FDR. I feel pretty certain he would have made more than one visit to the museum."

"Yes." She examined the photo again. "You would certainly think so."

Scoop took his phone and returned it to his coat pocket. "Maybe some of the staff will remember. Shirley was helpful." He apparently pumped her for information. I imagine there were others he spoke with at the museum or in town. "Don't worry about it." He brushed an errant curl back from her forehead. "You need to get some rest."

He stood abruptly. "I should go. I'll see you tomorrow at the museum?"

She nodded. "Yes." She rose and walked him to the back door. "I'll be there at eight, as usual."

"Good." He opened the door but turned back to her. "Does Teagan go to the museum with you when you're working?"

"When she isn't in school. She does her homework in my office and entertains herself around the grounds. Fergus watches over her." She smiled. "We live a very rural life here. The restrictions of the city don't always apply. The Director is very understanding."

He nodded and turned to leave but stopped again. "If you don't mind my asking, how did your husband die?"

Hannah's hand went to her throat. The question caught her off guard. She blinked, and took a step back.

"I'm sorry," Scoop said. "I'm sorry. I didn't mean to upset you." With that, he quickly disappeared down the steps and into the dense darkness of the night.

Hannah watched through the open door as the interior light of the car illuminated him for a brief moment then the engine and headlights sprang to life and he was backing away. She continued to watch until the tail lights disappeared down the road.

As she closed the door, she saw Callahan sitting, watching. It was as if he understood.

"I suppose I'll have to take you with us tomorrow morning, won't I?"

He blinked three times.

Chapter Seven

I won't deny that after a long day of sleuthing, I do love a good nap. All that talk about the nocturnal habits of felines is quite true but when you've been firing the old gray cells on the subject of murder, then a good long snooze on a comfy sofa is just the thing. Sad to say, there was little sleep to be had at the Sanderson house last night. The dog, Fergus, had a real flea in his ear about my presence. I can't imagine why. The sound of his nails tip-tapping along the hallway all through the night did not bode well for a cat with super sensitive hearing. If appearance is anything to go by, it didn't help Hannah much either.

Teagan is the only one who seems rested and ready to face a new day. And I am up to the challenge as well. A true mystery is begging to be solved and I won't let the mere lack of sleep divert me from the chase. Besides, the one thing that's more important than sleep to a cat, well, this cat, is a delicious breakfast to start the day. Rested or not, Hannah is no slouch in the kitchen. These scrambled eggs made with a large splash of whipping cream and a sprig of dill are a far cry from potted meat and saltine crackers. Not that I'm knocking potted meat and saltine crackers. I do believe I have fortified myself for whatever may come.

After tearing around the yard like a wild thing, Fergus has had his meal as well. What he ate is a mystery but, then, he's a dog. Hannah, for a human, was wise enough to opt for more familiar fare for me. Being a cat about town, I have my choice of fine dining. I'm thinking fried catfish at Bulloch's for lunch. Unless the clues take me elsewhere.

Neither Hannah nor Teagan had much of an appetite but I've noticed that strange occurrence often among the female of the species. They don't even listen to their own advice of a hearty breakfast to start the day. Their loss.

It would appear that we are headed to the museum. A teacher work day, whatever that may be, means Teagan won't return to the classroom until Monday. Whatever worries she may have experienced in the aftermath of the murder yesterday seem to have had no lasting effect. She is eager to get this show on the road.

Hannah makes a last circuit through the house, checking windows and the front door. With a last glance around the kitchen, she locks and double checks the back door. At last, we are off. Fergus and I have an understanding, of sorts. He has, wisely, decided to ride in the knee-well of the front seat with Teagan and I have the full range of the back seat from which to view the terrain.

The Sanderson house is a nifty spot in a little dip between hillocks with meadow grasses all around. One mighty oak stands at the back of the lawn. The rooftop of the nearest neighbor is visible on the top of one of those low hills but only just. As we pass by, the neighbor waves from the end of his driveway as he places mail into the box for pick up by the postman. Hannah gives a jaunty little double tap of *the horn in response.*

Ten minutes later, we pull onto Little White House Road. We stop to say good morning to Billy Brad before passing through the sawhorse blockade. I see that Scoop's car is already in the parking lot as are a patrol car and a couple of other vehicles that must belong to the staff. Two off-road vehicles that have the Park Service emblem on the doors are also here as well as a big rig that must have delivered them. My guess is Scoop has called in reinforcements.

When we enter Hannah's office, we find Scoop behind her desk leaning back in her chair. He rises as we enter.

"Good morning." *He runs a quick eye over both Hannah and Teagan.* "How was your night?"

Hannah gives him a hint of a smile and nods. "Fine. Thank you."

"All quiet?" *Scoop comes from behind the desk.*

"Of course." *Hannah glances at Teagan and places her purse on the desk with an emphatic thump.*

Scoop looks a little sheepish and holds up his phone. "I just wanted a little privacy to check in with Clay. They're running the fingerprints we collected at the scene but there are so many that it's like searching for a needle in a haystack."

"So, what now?"

"We've scheduled interviews with all the employees. I thought it would be better to do that here. In a familiar setting, things might be more easily remembered."

"Oh. Well, in that case, I suppose you'll be needing my office."

"No, that won't be necessary. The director has agreed to let us use the employee lounge."

The lounge. Good thinking. Much better to put people off their guard than the jailhouse with the thought of bars and locked doors lurking in everyone's thoughts. And the museum's break room is the center of all workplace gossip. Yes. Smart move.

Hannah looks around the office, her forehead creased with worry. "I don't really know what I can do with the museum shut down. I suppose it would have been better to stay at home."

"If you don't mind, I think it would be helpful to have you on hand. The employees will be more relaxed with you present."

"I won't have to sit in on the interviews, will I?" *I hear the apprehension in her voice.*

"Nothing like that but it might be helpful to check your recollection against what we learn."

She nods, then sits behind her desk, her hands idle. After a moment, she looks up at Scoop. "Right. Is there anything else you wanted to ask me?"

"Not now. I'll go over any concerns when we've finished with our interviews."

She nods and turns to Teagan. "We might as well take advantage of the time and get on with that book report due next week. Do you have it with you?"

Teagan drops her backpack to the floor. "What about the investigation?"

"Book report, young lady. The investigation is strictly off limits to you."

Teagan's disappointment is clear in her expression but she makes no reply. Just as well that Hannah put her foot down. A kid underfoot, even a budding junior sleuth like Teagan, is the last thing anyone needs is to be worried about. I mean, I like her well enough, considering my general inclination to steer clear of children, but my full attention has to be focused on finding the killer. Scoop's too, of course. And the CIRT team.

Hannah boots up her computer as Teagan settles at a small table in the corner and draws from the depths of her bookbag a book on none other than Roosevelt. His early years.

***

Scoop hesitated as Hannah logged onto her computer. He had the urge to say something more but wasn't sure what. After leaving her house the night before, he had called Clay and informed him about his concerns that Hannah had arrived home to find her back door unlocked. It was probably, as she said, that she had simply forgotten to lock it. Probably. Still, he felt better about the fact that the night shift would patrol the area. It concerned him that her house was so isolated.

Teagan had her book open but was watching him, hope evident in her expression. He gave her a wink and a smile as he turned from the room.

He poured himself a cup of coffee and settled at a table in the employee lounge. As he lifted the cup to his lips, he spied the gray cat slinking into the room. The cat glanced his way as if to say, nothing to see here, carry on as usual. Scoop smiled at the thought. He was becoming downright fanciful. With that, he put Callahan out of his mind and focused on the notes from his first interview of the day. One of the ticket takers remembered Curtis Arthur D'Amboise buying a ticket for the museum on more than one occasion over the past three weeks. She wasn't certain if it had been twice or three times.

That seemed logical. If the man was writing a book about Roosevelt, then more than one trip to the place that had featured so prominently in his life would be a given. The attendant had nothing further to offer about D'Amboise other than the fact he had flirted with her rather blatantly.

A fancy man, as the hotel manager had said.

Henry Wilkes was next on the list. He worked the grounds of the museum. Perhaps he would have something more useful to offer.

The man who took the chair across from Scoop had the look of a walnut. His face and hands were that dark and trenched with lines. He sat silently, staring straight at Scoop with rheumy blue eyes hazed by cataracts, his thumbs caught in the braces of his denim overalls.

"Mr. Wilkes, thanks for coming in."

No reply.

"You work maintenance of the grounds of the museum?"

Wilkes nodded.

Scoop remained silent but Wilkes felt no compulsion to comment further.

Scoop pushed the photo of Curtis Arthur D'Amboise across the table. "Do you recognize this man?"

Again, Wilkes nodded.

"Could you elaborate on that?"

"Nosy."

"How's that?"

"Poking 'round where he oughten. Asking questions."

"Poking around where?"

"Wandering in the woods. Looking in the sheds. Up to no good."

"Why do you say that?"

"The Gator parked in a different spot."

"Gator?"

Wilkes scowled. "Four wheeler. Used to haul stuff."

"Maybe you forgot where you parked it the day before."

"I don't forget."

"Anything else?"

"Things went missing."

"What things?"

"My scythe. Belonged to my grandpaw."

"You use a scythe?"

"Easier to use to get at the grass and weeds in close spaces and steep slopes. Quiet, too. Not all that loud noise the young'uns make with them weed eaters and such."

"When did it go missing?"

"Two, three days ago."

Scoop considered this. "You said nosy."

"Asking questions about the White House. About where to find any records of guests during the President's time there."

"What did you tell him?"

"I asked him if I looked like I knowed. Told him to leave where he don't belong. To ask folks up at the museum if he wanted to know such like."

"Anything else?"

For the first time, Wilkes looked away. Then he shook his head.

After a brief silence, Scoop asked, "How many times did you see him on the museum grounds?"

Wilkes rubbed his gnarled hands together, furrowed his brow with thought. "Three, four times." He looked up at Scoop. "Don't think he paid for a ticket regular-like."

"You think he slipped onto the museum grounds through the woods?"

"That would be my thinking."

"You didn't like him, did you?"

"I don't much like you, either. What of it?"

Scoop disguised a grunt of laughter with a cough. "Thanks for your time, Mr. Wilkes. If I have any more questions, where can I find you?"

"Working. Weeds don't pay no never mind to man or the law."

With that, Henry Wilkes stood and left the room. As he passed through the door, Teagan appeared. He gave her a pat on the head and continued on his way.

Teagan stood on the threshold of the room, Fergus at her side. "I need a drink of water."

"Help yourself." Scoop stood and moved with his cup of coffee to the window overlooking the paved walkways of the outer circle of the museum complex. "Do you spend a lot of time at the museum, Teagan?"

She came to stand beside him and look out the window. "Yes, sir."

"You must know it pretty well, then."

She looked up at him. "I do."

"I bet you see a lot that goes on around here."

Her brow furrowed. "I guess so."

"What do you think of Mr. Wilkes?"

"I like him."

"Yeah?"

"He helps me with my history homework. And geography."

"Does he?"

She nodded. "He knows all kinds of things. He can name every tree and every bird and every insect."

"I would never have guessed it."

"He's quiet. He doesn't much like people. Except for me. And Fergus."

"He seems very old to still be working."

"I suppose. But he's worked here all his life. Well, since he was my age, anyway."

"Really?"

She nodded. "He knows everything there is to know about President Roosevelt."

"That must come in handy with your homework."

"Yes. But he teaches me other things, too."

"Like what?"

She remained silent for a moment. "Patience. How to be quiet and listen."

"Good qualities to have."

She looked up at him then turned to the mini fridge and took out a bottle of water. "I can help you find clues," she said from the open doorway.

"I think that would worry your mother."

Her forehead creased into a furrow and she nodded before turning down the hallway.

* * *

Hannah watched Teagan enter her office and slump into the chair where her school books waited. She toyed with the water bottle she had gotten in the break room but didn't open it. An excuse, Hannah decided, to have a word with Scoop. It had been a mistake to bring her to the museum. She wondered how long she would need to be on hand. The best thing for her and Teagan would be to stay as far away from the investigation as possible.

Hannah had intended for Teagan to spend the day in the museum shop with Shirley while Hannah met her friends for a leisurely lunch at Callaway Gardens. The murder had disrupted all that and Hannah had concerns about leaving

Teagan to her own devices. She seemed drawn to the puzzle of the dead man in the servants' quarters. And to Scoop.

The four sorority sisters would have to change their plans. Hannah decided lunch at The Bulloch House Restaurant would be a better option. That way she could be close to the museum if she was needed. She glanced at the clock on the wall. It wasn't yet nine o'clock. She'd wait until nine-thirty to call the girls. That way, she wouldn't disturb the late sleepers. She sighed. Lunch seemed an eternity away.

The phone on her desk rang. "Hannah Sanderson," she said as she answered it.

"Ms. Sanderson, this is Chase Gibbons with *The LaGrange Daily News*. I'm calling to get a statement about the dead body at the museum."

Hannah was stunned speechless by the request. Because of their late night, she didn't know if information about the murder had run on the nightly news. It hadn't occurred to her that the museum would be called upon to give a statement.

"Ms. Sanderson?"

"Oh. Sorry. You caught me off guard. You'll need to speak with the director of the museum. Let me see if he's in his office."

"Already tried that. He's out of the office for the day."

"I see." Her thoughts were spinning wildly. What to do? "I'm sure the Warm Springs police department can give you whatever information you need. I don't know much about what happened and haven't been authorized to discuss it. With anyone."

"I understand some kids found the body."

"You need to check with the police department. I'm

sure you have their number."

"Come on, Ms. Sanderson. Just a yes or no. What would that hurt?"

"I'm afraid I can't help you Mr.—"

"Gibbons. Chase Gibbons. Look, let me give you my number and if you change your mind—"

"I won't change my mind, Mr. Gibbons. If you want information you need to go through the proper channels."

"The whole town's talking about it."

"Then why are you asking me?"

"I need facts not gossip."

"I don't have the facts. Call the police department." She hung up the phone.

Hannah felt flushed and her heart was racing. What now? The fact that the murder had taken place on the premises of the Little White House would be newsworthy, if only for a short span of the news cycle. It might even attract national interest. Would they be under siege from a host of news outlets? She needed to talk to Scoop.

"I'll be right back," she said to Teagan.

All that garnered was a glance before Teagan returned her full attention to her iPad.

Scoop was leaning against the window casing and staring out at the museum grounds when she entered the employees' lounge. When he looked over his shoulder and saw her, he straightened and came back to the table he was using as a desk and set his Styrofoam cup down.

"We've established that the victim was on the premises multiple times over the course of the past two to three weeks. Are you sure you don't remember seeing him?"

"I'm not at all sure that I didn't see him but I don't recall *seeing* him. Do you know what I mean?"

"Yes. Maybe you could take a look at this photo that I

received this morning. It's from his Florida driver's license." He handed her the picture from a file jacket.

Hannah studied it then shook her head. "I'm sorry. I honestly don't recognize him."

Scoop nodded and returned the photo to the file.

"There's something else you need to know," Hannah said. "A reporter just called my office. He wants a statement about the dead body."

"Is that how he worded it? The dead body?"

"Yes."

"Good. At least no one is asking about the murder yet. I was nailed at breakfast by a kid from a local weekly asking the same. The story was on the Atlanta news this morning. Let's hope that's all the notice we get. Warm Springs isn't exactly a hot spot of interest."

"You don't think the fact that the body was found at the museum will be newsworthy?"

"It's newsworthy but only if there's nothing much going on elsewhere. We can only hope that whoever spilled the beans hasn't gone higher up the food chain to a major network."

Scoop's phone rang and he looked at the number before answering. "Yes, Birdie."

He was silent as he listened. Then he sighed. "Tell them our agency is called in anytime there's a death on park property. That at the moment it's a preliminary investigation into cause of death and when we have more facts, we'll release a statement."

Scoop hung up and looked across the table at Hannah. "Someone's been talking to the press."

"The reporter said everyone in town is talking about it."

"So far, the cause of death hasn't leaked. Let's try to keep it that way."

"What caused his death? Do you know?"

"A blow to the back of the head with a blunt object. Something substantial."

"Maybe it was an accident. From a fall, perhaps?"

Scoop shook his head. "As much as I'd like that to be the case, you and I know better. It's a body in a locked room. Someone placed him there."

Hannah frowned. Wishful thinking wasn't going to change the facts. "What should we do?"

"Be careful in your interaction with everyone. One wrong word about the circumstances and we'll have a full-blown news event. How much do you trust the staff? Oscar? Shirley?"

"I can warn them not to say anything."

"That's a double-edged sword. Sometimes that serves to heighten the desire to tell. Do either of them suspect it was murder?"

"They're not stupid. The room was sealed from the outside."

"It's only a matter of time then."

"What should we do?"

Scoop thought for a moment. "My team will deflect any questions put to them. We'll prepare a response for the questions that will come. Tell your staff to refer all inquiries to either you, Clay, or me."

"Should I tell them not to reveal what they know?"

"It's probably too late for that but you can try."

"And what, exactly, should I say to any questions?"

"That the museum has turned the matter over to the CIRT team of the state parks' law enforcement division. A body was found on the premises but you have no further details."

"The reporter knew that it was discovered by children."

"Well, that should certainly be fodder for sensationalizing the matter."

Hannah hugged her waist. "I'm worried about Teagan. I don't want her to become a target for an aggressive reporter."

"Keep her close. Tell her not to talk to anyone."

Hannah nodded. His advice didn't allay her concerns but it appeared to be the only actionable choice she had.

Chapter Eight

Scoop is quite right about the power of secrets. To know someone's secret is to have power over them. This knowledge makes people feel superior, special, sought after. Powerful. Like me, only my superiority is due to my finely honed senses and skills. And a lifetime of fending for myself has taught me what makes humans tick.

What? You think I'm tooting my own horn? I could write a book on their behavior, which to the untrained eye, can be majorly bi-polar at times. They can often act in ways that are totally against their best interest. Unlike cats who always do exactly what they want. And if a cat's actions seem inscrutable to a human, it's because they don't torture themselves with self-doubt and hidden agendas.

But secrets can also create unexpected consequences. Like murder.

Right now, Hannah is being hounded by the press. They will dig under the skin of the corpse of Curtis Arthur D'Amboise in the hopes of revealing something spectacular, attention grabbing, shocking. The fact that the good citizens of Warm Springs are spreading the news that children are in-the-know puts Teagan at risk. A problem, yes. What to do?

I think I'd better check on her. She's drawn to the investigation. Anyone could trick her into revealing details. Hannah is concerned that she might be used by a scalawag of a reporter. Though he hides it well, I can tell that Scoop has concerns along these lines as well. And, like me, he's aware that it might draw the attention of our killer.

It's no secret that Teagan spends a lot of time on the museum grounds. If the murderer decides she's seen or knows something about this death then she can be in real danger. It tarnishes the shine of the chase a bit, this newfound concern for a human. And a child-human at that. I suppose it's because this is my first actual murder. Well, other than that Annoying Rooster at the farm down by the railroad tracks. The Farmer is convinced it was a fox. I'm not so sure. The Retired Postman seems to be enjoying sleeping in these days. Sometimes the obvious is the answer. As I said, humans tend to complicate things.

The half dozen employees who have been interviewed this morning have had little information of value beyond the fact that Curtis Arthur D'Amboise has been spending time in and around the museum and that he was smarmy and nosy. Curtis Arthur D'Amboise. What a moniker! I think I'll save a little brain power and call him what he really is, a Punk. Yeah, The Punk. Perfect. From what we've discovered so far, it suits him down to the ground.

It's unfortunate that Scoop is so pig-headed about following my lead. I'm still trying to figure out whether last night's need to remove me from The Punk's hotel room was a flat-out dismissal of my usefulness or an excuse to go in search of the lovely Hannah. Either way, it's a good thing that he acted on the itch, whatever the motivation.

Hannah's unlocked door bothers me. She doesn't strike me as the type to forget, regardless of the peace and sense of safety the countryside of Georgia implies. Agatha Christie knew a thing or two about the dark side of country life. Just ask Lil, the Librarian. Perhaps that's who Teagan should be reading rather than the life of Roosevelt, which, apparently, is spoon fed to the local population from birth and is, therefore, well known to her.

But, what's this? The office is empty. Teagan and Fergus are not here.

As she enters the office on my heels, Hannah comes to an abrupt halt. "Teagan," *she whispers. She does an about face and heads for the shop. No one is there. Abruptly she turns and hurries back to the employees' lounge.* "Have you seen Teagan? She's gone."

Scoop crosses the room to Hannah. "She was here earlier."

Hannah wrings her hands, a frightened look on her face.

"Calm down," *he says.*

"She's gone! I left her in the office and now—"

"Where would she go? Is the dog with her?"

A look of relief washes over Hannah's features and she closes her eyes briefly. "Fergus. She probably took Fergus for a walk." *She shakes her head.* "I guess I'm not thinking clearly."

"A walk. That sounds logical." *Scoop slips his arm around Hannah's waist as he turns her toward the hallway.* "Let's go have a look. She can't have gone far."

I'm glad that Scoop is able to reassure Hannah but I'm not so certain. I get the impression that Teagan knows the grounds like the back of her hand. She could be anywhere. And she's on a mission. Her sharp mind is obsessed with the complexity of the case. I understand that feeling, the burning desire to figure-it-out. Whether it's how to get the last taste of Dinty Moore's Beef Stew from the bottom of the can, to manipulate the loose door on the heated greenhouse to avoid the bite of winter wind, or to catch a thief in the act and guilt him into sharing a bit of the snatched sweet roll, it's all about getting to the bottom of the situation. And, let's face it, a dead body in a locked room would capture anyone's imagination. Yes, she's off in search of clues, or I'm the Mad Hatter.

* * *

Over a lifetime of playing baseball, Scoop had honed certain skills. Of particular use in his current life was the ability to infer future action by the incremental ticks and adjustments observable in body movements. Watching the batter, he learned to anticipate the direction of the ball strike. It gave him that split-second advantage to determine the trajectory of the ball and put himself in its path. The same theory could be applied to human behavior in general.

He didn't need those skills to know that Teagan was most likely headed to the servants' quarters in search of clues. It was the kind of thing an inquisitive child would do. Her presence at the museum was problematic. She didn't need to be in the center of the crime scene but he didn't think he should voice that concern to Hannah at the moment. She was already wound tight with worry.

In truth, he was concerned as well. It was impossible to completely secure the scene. The large wooded area that surrounded the museum grounds could be penetrated from many directions and from a profusion of cover.

Hannah seemed to have read his mind. She headed straight across the outer circle to the guard gates and the servants' quarters just below. There was no sign of Teagan and the dog.

That panicked expression as she hurried across the patio and looked up and down the inner circle drive that ran in front of the Little White House grew as there was no evidence of the child anywhere.

"Teagan!" she called.

There was no answer.

She turned toward Scoop. "Where could she be?"

He placed a calming hand on her shoulder. "Think. Where does she routinely walk the dog?"

Hannah raced up the steps, around the bumper gates, and toward the building that housed the public bathrooms. Beyond them was an area of partially cleared terrain.

"She brings him behind here away from the public areas."

But, as they rounded the corner of the building they were met with serene quiet. Before them was a sparsely wooded area that petered out into the surrounding denser growth. Nothing stirred, not even a squirrel.

Scoop saw the desperation on Hannah's face. He took out his phone and dialed.

"Mac, we're looking for Teagan. Have you or any of your team seen her?" He waited as McFadden inquired.

"One of the volunteers saw her headed toward the creek along what he called Rabbit Run," Scoop said to Hannah.

"Rabbit Run?"

Hannah, who had been watching him intently, started off in an easterly direction. Scoop let her get a few yards ahead of him before asking McFadden "Was she alone?"

"No. She was with a man."

"What about the dog?"

McFadden called out the question to the man who had seen Teagan.

"No," he said.

"Head that way. We may have a problem."

* * *

Hannah felt the panic taking over but she focused on the path ahead. After David's death she went through a period of months where she was prone to panic attacks. With time, they had abated. She felt the breathlessness rising, the sweating and chills. She couldn't let it take hold. Teagan might be in danger.

She began to run. Please, God, she silently prayed. Please.

Suddenly, Scoop was beside her with a long, loping stride, the gray cat outpacing them both. He made no attempt to reassure her, to shush her concerns, which, in its own way was a comfort.

Rabbit Run was exactly that, a path through the woods running down to a little creek. Often, in the early morning or very late afternoon, brown rabbits appeared along the length of it to nibble the tender grasses that grew there.

She could hear the sound of running feet off to her right approaching at an intersect angle.

McFadden and two other men burst through the dense foliage just as Hannah and Scoop reached the end of the path at the creek bank.

There, sitting on a large slab of stone that protruded from the earth and overhung the water tumbling over the pebble strewn stream bed, was Teagan. She wasn't alone.

As the five adults burst onto the scene, Henry Wilkes looked over his shoulder and gave them a long look before returning his attention to the red and white cork bobbing on the water.

"Teagan!" Hannah was out of breath and on the verge of tears with relief. "What are you doing down here?"

"Fergus wanted to go out."

"You should have told me!" Hannah realized her voice sounded sharp but fear had given way to anger. It was irrational, she knew, but there it was.

"But I never tell you." Teagan looked stricken by her mother's response.

Hannah placed her hand on her forehead and exhaled a calming breath. "I know. I know." She caught Teagan's hand and pulled her to her feet where she then wrapped her in a tight hug. "Sorry, Bean."

Teagan returned the embrace. "I'm sorry, Mom."

"It's okay." She gave Scoop a *mea culpa* smile. "I think I've had too much coffee this morning."

Teagan leaned her head back until she could look Hannah in the eye. "It's the murder. But you shouldn't be scared. We'll catch him." She cast Scoop a knowing side eye.

Fergus climbed the shallow bank of the creek, water dripping from his coat. "Woof."

Callahan flattened his ears then proceeded to groom his paw. Hannah couldn't help but smile. Both cat and dog had decided it was all much ado about nothing.

Chapter Nine

I confess, Teagan scared the bejeezus out of everyone, including me. She has a head on her shoulders, that one, but there's a killer out there somewhere and until he's caught, everyone will be on edge. A child would be helpless against the murderer if he thought she posed a threat.

Hannah's fear is understandable. Everyone thinks crime happens in big cities, not sleepy little towns like Warm Springs. Especially when it comes to murder.

I hope Scoop is ready to move on from the museum. His team has that under control. The Punk's hotel room holds the key, I'm sure of it. Call it a cat's intuition, or a tingling of my Spidey senses, or revelations from the Great Karnack. Whatever. I prefer to think of it as channeling Sam Spade. Besides, I wouldn't say no to a nice dish of peach ice cream right about now.

It seems, for once, Scoop is on the same wavelength. Now that he has Hannah and Teagan safely settled in Hannah's office at the museum, he's headed toward his car. Now, the tricky part. How to hitch a ride. He has made himself clear on his view of my talents so I'll just have to make headway on my own while using him to extract what information he can.

He opens the car door just as his phone rings. While he is preoccupied with the call, I slip inside and over the backrest to secure a ride on the floorboard of the back seat. Humiliating, I know, but a cat must do what a cat must do for the sake of the case.

The ride is short so as the car comes to a stop, I know we must be in the heart of the little town. And I'm right. When Scoop opens the car door, I slither from my hiding place and squeeze through the opening between seat and door frame to land on the pavement of Broad Street in front of The Bulloch House Restaurant. It seems our flatfoot is hungry. So am I, but I must ignore the rumblings of my tummy and take advantage of the time I have while Scoop is occupied.

Traffic consists of one lone car cruising slowly down the street. I sprint across the roadway and up the steps to the storefronts on the other side. It's nice and shady here under the over-hangings and awnings of the businesses that lead to the hotel that is the anchor of the business district. There isn't any pedestrian traffic and the whole area resonates with that quiet of the lunch time lull.

Upon arrival at the hotel, I find the door firmly closed. But, I'm in luck. Only a few steps away, the door of the ice cream parlor opens as a young woman exits with a cone piled high with a delicious-looking frozen concoction. I take advantage of the opportunity and sprint inside just as the door closes.

Behind the counter, a young woman is busy with her arm elbow deep in a freezer so I resist the mouth-watering aroma of freshly baked waffle cones and slip through the doorway into the hotel lobby.

No one's in sight. I'm free to familiarize myself with the items on the reception desk and the hotel's switchboard. It's a fascinating piece of equipment but I can't linger to explore. I must make hay while I have the freedom to roam the premises.

In an alcove under the stairs is a closed door. It leads to the functional rooms of the hotel but again, I'm denied access. That leaves the rooms above and the true goal of this excursion. The Punk's room.

My superior hearing detects the sound of stealthy movement above. I race up the stairs on silent paws in search of the source. Down the hallway and on the left almost to the very back of the hotel is The Punk's room. A woman is kneeling down, attempting to look through the keyhole and it isn't Alice. In fact, it's a very pretty young woman with a mass of chestnut hair. And when I say young, I mean late teens. Certainly no older than twenty. There is something familiar about her.

She tries the door knob and at the noise it makes, she glances quickly down the hallway. At the sight of me, she springs to her feet. A quick glancing search beyond me reassures her that she is safe.

She tries the door knob again but much more aggressively this time. She casts another glance in my direction, the look on her face is one of fear and frustration. A door closes below stairs and the frustration is replaced by fright. She races to the back of the hallway and through a door.

I race to catch up with her and spy a staircase just as the door closes in my face. Thwarted again.

Who is this young beauty and what is her interest in The Punk? Or, more importantly, his room?

I change course to the front of the hotel and down the stairs. Alice looks up from a stack of mail she is sorting as I paw at the door.

"What's this?" *she asks.* "You want to go out?" *She comes from behind the registration desk.* "How did you get in here in the first place?"

A dash through the inner passageways of the hotel would be the surest means to catch the intruder but there's no time to delay by trying to communicate my need to the hotel manager.

She eyes me, hands on hips, as if she's not quite certain whether to be annoyed or not. I frantically paw at the door. Time is of the essence. Finally, she opens it.

I race through the door, past the Tuscawilla Soda Shop, and down the narrow side porch of the hotel that fronts the parking lot in the hopes of catching up with our snoop.

I am too late. Where could she have disappeared to so quickly? I lope along the rear of the businesses that adjoin the hotel, past jutting add-ons, stacked crates, and other oddities of shopkeepers best kept out of sight of customers. My hope is to get a glimpse of the Mysterious Lady of the Hallway.

All of the back doors of these establishments are firmly closed. I come to the alleyway that runs straight through to the main street. It's very narrow and decorated with whimsical art on the stepping stones but quite passable for pedestrians.

As I emerge onto the sidewalk of Broad Street, I check both directions in search of my prey. Whoever the young lady is, she's long gone. I'm discouraged but not defeated. The little gray cells will find the memory of her. Besides, I'm hungry. Perhaps it's time I checked out The Bulloch House Restaurant. It justifiably has quite the reputation and draws diners from all over Meriwether and Harris counties. I'm sure I'll be able to seduce one of the staff into indulging me with a little treat. I am, after all, quite adorable when I choose to be and there is always a soft touch among the workers.

* * *

Scoop followed the waitress as she threaded her way through the tables of diners. The Bulloch House Restaurant was bustling with the noon rush. As they paused to allow a large table of patrons to make their way past, he overheard the tail end of a comment.

"...that's when Eubie threatened him with that shotgun he keeps behind the counter."

Scoop looked over at a four square where three men who had long since qualified for Medicare sat lingering over their dessert. He touched the waitress lightly on the arm and asked in a low voice if he could have the table near them.

She frowned at his request but gave a nod and began clearing it of the last patron's lunch debris. Scoop settled in with his back at an angle to the old timers.

"Aw, heck, Woodrow, Eubie ain't shot nobody. He probably ain't ever shot anything with that gun. Can't see two feet in front of his face."

"He gets a kick out of pulling out that old double barrel and pointing it at folks that annoy him," one of the other men at the table responded.

The third man at the table gave a snort of laughter. "Besides, ain't nobody said he was shot, now have they?"

"No way he was shot. The director lives right there near the property. He'd a heard it. 'Specially if it was a shotgun."

"All I'm sayin'," prompted the original speaker, "is that this was murder. Mark my words."

"Why in tarnation would anyone in Warm Springs want to shoot him?" asked the voice of reason.

"Why would anybody want to kill anyone? The heat. The humidity. Road rage. Folks don't need a reason these days." The original speaker had his mind made up and Scoop conceded that the rest of the town would soon be thinking the same thing.

A different waitress came to take his order. She looked harried, loose curls escaping from the combs holding her hair back, and her face flushed. "Sorry about the wait, hon. What can I get you?"

"Is it always this busy?"

She glanced around the restaurant. "It's a little more than usual but folks are traveling these days since the pandemic is behind us. School will be out in another week." She grinned. "Folks gotta eat."

"And I hear this is the best place to do just that."

Her smile widened. "You got that right. We're pushed today because we're short-handed. Charlene didn't show up." She shook her head. "Kids. No sense of responsibility. Didn't call or anything. All she can think about is Nashville."

"Yeah?"

"Wants to be a country singer. Always videoing herself singing and picking at places around the county. Says it adds dramatic effect and shows off our uniqueness. Posts them on Facebook and TikTok, whatever that is."

"Can she sing?"

"Like a nightingale."

"Well, good luck to her."

Scoop placed his order and gave the waitress the menu. The old men at the next table had moved on to the subject of teenagers spray painting a barn with graffiti. Scoop watched the patrons and let his mind wander to the case. From the corner of his eye, he saw a man table-hopping. The people at the tables he visited didn't appear to know him but warmed to him over the course of each brief exchange. Scoop recognized him for what he was. A reporter.

He turned so his back was to the man. The last thing he wanted was to be identified. He took out his notebook and read through the details he'd jotted down in his personal shorthand code. A notation gave him pause. What had he meant by those brief letters? He thought about it then remembered. As he was putting the notebook away, something else occurred to him. Curtis D'Amboise had just such a code on the tablet on the desk in his room. They needed to figure out what it meant.

The waitress returned with his meal and he tucked in. The fried chicken was crispy and cooked to perfection. Everything else was just as tasty. He gave a thought to McFadden and Birdie scouring the museum compound in the sweltering heat and experienced a fleeting moment of guilt as he finished off the last bite of lemon pie.

At that moment, two things happened. Hannah and her sorority sisters entered the restaurant and his phone rang.

Hannah became aware of his presence and quickly looked away.

The phone call was from the Pine Mountain police. They had another dead body.

Scoop rose abruptly and took out his wallet. He dropped cash enough to pay for his meal and leave a generous tip onto the table. Rather than getting caught up in an encounter with Hannah, he turned toward the rear of the restaurant and found the exit near the kitchen. On the small porch the gray cat was finishing up what looked like a dish of fried catfish.

Callahan looked up when Scoop opened the door and

immediately fell in behind him as he rounded the building headed for his car. At the moment, the inscrutable behavior of the cat was the least of his concerns so Scoop made no objection when the cat hopped into the car the moment the door opened and took up the shotgun position.

* * *

Hannah glanced back at the table where she'd seen Scoop. It was empty. She silently chastised herself for her knee-jerk reaction to seeing him. She wasn't a college co-ed anymore so why had she acted like one?

She looked out the glass panel of the door of the restaurant to check on Teagan, who was helping Alice water the ferns and flowers in the pots in front of the hotel. She saw Scoop get into his car, back out of the parking space, and speed away like his tail was on fire. The heat traveled up her neck and face. How humiliating!

The lunch crowd was beginning to thin and a waitress settled them at a table that offered them a bit of privacy from the remaining patrons. They were discussing the merits of the various entrees when a man who looked to be in his mid-thirties approached their table.

"Hello, ladies. Are you locals?"

Jackie caught Hannah's eye then looked up at the intruder. "Tourists. Staying at Callaway Gardens. What's good on the menu?"

"I haven't eaten yet," he replied, his thoughts already on the next table over as he spoke, "but I hear everything's good."

"Great," Jackie said. "That means there are no wrong choices."

"Have a nice lunch, ladies," he replied and moved on.

Once he was out of earshot, Hannah asked, "How did you know?"

"Well, he was either the owner, in which case he would recognize you, or he's a reporter looking for background and gossip."

"Thanks," Hannah said.

Jackie shrugged. "What are friends for?"

Phyllis piped in, "They're to cheer you up."

"Yes," Sue said. "Let's plan on a round of golf tomorrow to get your mind off things. I hear Teagan has become quite the little golfer."

"Sounds like fun for you guys," Phyllis said, "but count me out. I have a good book and I'm not about to risk turning into one giant freckle. I'll meet all of you at the clubhouse afterwards."

"Spoilsport," her three companions chimed in unison.

"That may be, but I have a hot date with a dreamboat for the office Memorial Day picnic next weekend."

Everyone laughed. Phyllis had always been the delicate flower of the foursome. All her life it had been pounded into her head by her mother that she must protect her delicate, creamy white skin. Throughout their friendship all outdoor activities had been fraught with peril for Phyllis's fair complexion. Lotions, hats, and umbrellas had been *de rigueur* for any such occasion.

The planning for the next two days took the friends through a leisurely lunch. Hannah kept her mind squarely in the moment. But when the three women climbed back into Phyllis's SUV, Hannah let her thoughts stray to the situation at the museum.

The upcoming Memorial Day weekend saw a lot of

tourist traffic. What would they do if the museum remained off limits because of the unresolved murder? And, if it did, would that draw more media attention?

In less than a week's time, people would be lined up to go through the exhibit and the museum couldn't afford to lose the revenue. Funding was always tight but the pandemic had wreaked havoc with the state budget. Every facility had to pull its own weight. The consequences didn't bear thinking about. Jobs and lives had already been lost due to Covid. Hannah had managed because of the benefits she received from the government due to David's death. The museum supported so many more than those employed to run it. The community was just getting back on its feet. What would happen to Warm Springs without the tourists the museum drew? A media frenzy could only make matters worse.

As if the gods were privy to her thoughts, Hannah looked down Broad Street in anticipation of crossing over to the hotel. There, crawling along the main thoroughfare of Warm Springs, was the WXIA news van.

The moment the street was clear, Hannah rushed across to the hotel. She found Teagan and Fergus in the Tuscawilla Soda Shop watching Alice as she turned out a tray of fudge.

"Thanks, Alice, for entertaining Teagan. I'll take her off your hands now." Hannah tried to hide the urgency she felt. She didn't want Teagan to encounter the news team. She glanced out the front window and saw that the van had pulled into the gas station near the intersection. "We're going to Callaway to take a dip in the pool." She eyed the fudge and reached into her purse. "How about a half dozen squares to take to the girls?"

Alice looked up at Hannah and her eyes narrowed ever so slightly. "Go wash up, Teagan. You're sticky to your elbows."

The moment the two women heard the distant sound of the bathroom door closing, Alice said, "What?"

"A news crew just got into town. I don't want them to get anywhere near Teagan."

Alice nodded. "I guess they'll go on out to the museum."

"Billy Brad will turn them away."

"Then I expect I'll be next."

"Probably."

She nodded again. "Well, forewarned is forearmed." She rang up Hannah's purchase and gave her change. "You should probably give that detective a heads up."

Hannah hesitated. "Probably."

They heard Teagan's approaching footsteps. "Best hurry along," Alice said.

"Right." Hannah took the box of fudge and the trio of mother, daughter, and dog hurried to the car.

They were buckled in. Hannah had backed out of the parking space in front of the hotel and headed east. Teagan turned to look into the back seat to see that Fergus was settled. "Look, Mom. It's the television station."

Hannah glanced in the rearview mirror. "Uh huh."

Teagan faced her mother. "They're here about the murder."

"Possibly."

"Is that why we're going swimming at Callaway?" Hannah looked at her daughter and gave a shake of her head as she smiled. "Aren't you the smart one."

"I wouldn't tell any of the clues."

"I know, Bean, but it's best if we simply avoid them as

long as we can. These people don't know us and all they care about is a headline. They can be very pushy. And, they can twist your words to fit the story they want to tell."

Unbidden thoughts of the media camping out on the lane leading to her house in the aftermath of David's capture in Afghanistan caused Hannah to avert her face and increase her speed. She would not allow Teagan to be subjected to such ruthlessness again.

Teagan stared straight ahead, that serious expression on her face, and lapsed into silence.

Chapter Ten

I'm not sure what has Scoop in such a rush. He's taking these curves hell bent for leather. It's true I have nine lives but I like the one I'm living right now, thank you very much. Let's hope we don't go careening off the mountainside in our mad dash to wherever.

I know I'm always smug about figuring out what motivates the people who wander onto my turf, but Cool Hand Luke is a different kettle of fish. He doesn't even talk to himself which would be a great help about now. Something has us racing up Pine Mountain and I hope it's more than a desire for muscadine jelly at The Country Kitchen.

His phone rings through the speakers and he pushes a button on the steering wheel. McFadden's voice fills the car.

"Got a problem, Boss."

"What?"

"A news crew is down at the blockade and the kid manning it is enjoying his fifteen minutes of fame."

Scoop bangs the palm of his hand against the steering wheel. "I thought Billy Brad was more professional than that."

"It isn't Billy Brad."

"Then who the heck is it?"

"Someone with the volunteer fire department. Said Bishop needed Billy Brad on something else."

"Pine Mountain must have contacted him. There's another body. Just below Dowdell's Knob. I'm on my way there now. I'll need you and Birdie."

Well, at least now I know why I'm risking life and limb in this mad race to reach the mountain top.

"What about the news crew?"

Scoop is silent for such a long time that McFadden prompts him again.

"Boss?"

"Send Birdie down to give a statement. Put the kid to combing the woods where the old guy said the scythe went missing. Maybe a little sweating in the heat and thickets will teach him to hold his tongue. See if the museum has someone to man the barricade until we can get reinforcements from Atlanta. We're going to need them. We have bodies in two different jurisdictions. At this point, we can't worry about the press. The cat's out of the bag, or it soon will be."

I'm not sure how I feel about that reference. Is it a good thing or a bad thing for the cat to be out of the bag? Who wouldn't want the cat out of the bag when it comes to murder? Is this one of those peculiarities of human speech meant to confuse and deflect?

Suddenly, we're making a sharp turn off the roadway and down a shady dirt lane. As we navigate the twists and turns of the wooded lane, it opens up. Ahead in a parking lay-by are two vehicles and a patrol car with lights flashing. Scoop drives past the statue of FDR sitting and overlooking the view, past the flagpole where the stars and stripes are barely moving in the mountain air. We stop on the lip of the ridge with the spectacular view overlooking the valley below. There's not a cloud in the sky. If not for the blue lights flashing, one could never imagine that death awaits us.

Scoop puts the car in park and pauses for one last direction to McFadden.

"Pack up your gear and get over here."

A kid in jeans, sturdy hiking boots, with a backpack resting at his feet, watches us as we get out of the car. He spares me a glance then, with a jerk of his thumb, indicates the edge of the precipice.

"He's down there."

"Did you find him?" *Scoop and I look over the drop-off. We can see two men positioned near an outcropping. One is in a police uniform. Near him, a man's leg and foot are visible through the dense, low vegetation. The rest of the body is hidden by a large pillar of rock protruding from the mountainside. It overshadows a goat trail leading downward.*

The kid answers. "It was the shoe. It has reflective stripes. The sun caught it. That's what got my attention. I could see it was someone down there."

"Did you climb down?"

He nods.

"And?"

"He's dead."

"You're sure?"

The kid looks kind of green. He turns his head away and clears his throat. "Been dead a while."

Scoop eyes him, then with a jerk of his head indicates the shady picnic area sitting back from the precipice. "Why don't you go sit up there? Someone will take your statement as soon as possible."

With a nod, the kid picks up his backpack and heads to a picnic table.

During this exchange, the policeman has been making his way up the precarious trail leading from the body. Scoop reaches out and clasps his hand to help him over the last bit of the incline.

"What do we have?"

The policeman dusts his hands together then runs the back of his forearm across his sweaty brow. "Middle aged male, partially bald, about five ten, I'd say. No ID."

"How long has he been dead?"

The policeman shakes his head. "Hard to say. Forty-eight hours or more would be my guess. The heat hasn't helped."

Scoop glances toward the picnic area where the young man is sitting with his head in his hands. It doesn't take a rocket scientist to visualize what he saw.

"Cause of death? Was it an accident?"

"Can't say that either. He suffered blunt force trauma to the head. He's all scratched and scraped. The head wound is deep. There're signs of blood along the drop but they're minor. Could have gotten there from a fall. Maybe."

"Maybe?"

The officer put his hands on his hips and sighs as he looks out over the valley. "The wound was deep. Could have happened if he hit that protrusion head on, I suppose."

"You're thinking it might not be accidental?"

He shrugs. "That's above my pay grade. It's the coroner's call. Odd though."

"Why's that?"

"If he hit his head on the outcropping, there wouldn't be any blood on the descent, would there? And there would be blood at the impact point of the boulder." *He gives Scoop an appraising look.* "You got here fast."

"I was in Warm Springs."

"Oh, yeah. The museum murder."

"Who said it was murder?"

"Everybody. A body in a sealed room. It's not rocket science."

Scoop doesn't reply. I know what he's thinking. Do we have a serial killer on our hands? Both victims died from a blow to the head. While both lawmen are preoccupied, I'd best take advantage of the opportunity and have a look for myself. And what's with this rocket science everyone keeps talking about? I bet Lil would know.

* * *

Hannah pulled into the long drive that led to her house. She could see a patrol car parked near the carport. She gave a mental sigh. The last thing she needed was an awkward dance around Clay's pursuit tactics.

As she got out of her car, Billy Brad appeared from around the corner of the house. She did a double take and a mental recalculation.

"Hey, Billy Brad."

He lifted his hand in an abbreviated wave as he approached.

"What are you doing here?"

He gestured toward the security lights mounted on the corners of the carport. "Clay wanted me to take a look at the lights. He's worried about you being out here on your own."

Hannah tamped down on the knee-jerk reaction that sprang to her mind. While it was thoughtful of Clay to be concerned for her safety, the presumption was irritating. She forced a smile. "That's good of you, Billy Brad."

"No trouble. I'm pretty good with my hands, especially electrical things. Worked with my cousin in his repair business before I joined the force."

"I'm sure that comes in handy."

He nodded and looked up at the lights. "I think I've solved the problem. But, if you have any more issues, just let me know."

At that point, Teagan opened the back door for Fergus to get out of the car.

He immediately ran toward Billy Brad with a stiff legged trot. At about two feet out, he stopped and woofed then made a circle around the police officer.

Billy Brad tried to engage the Scottie but Fergus was having none of it. He returned to Teagan and stood in a rigid stance between her and the law officer, his body aquiver.

"That's some watch dog you got there," Billy Brad said.

Hannah couldn't understand Fergus' behavior. He was usually so well-mannered. "It's the tension in the air, I think. He's very sensitive to human emotions."

"And I'm on his turf. Dogs can be territorial. I'm glad for the both of you that he's around." He let his gaze travel over the landscape from hilltop to hilltop. His cell phone began to make that muted vibrating sound. He checked the number but didn't answer. "I'll be off. Looks like Clay needs me."

Hannah shaded her eyes against the sun and looked up at the lights of the carport. She worried she had sounded ungrateful. "Thanks, again, Billy Brad. I really do appreciate it."

"Any time."

He climbed into his vehicle and made a big loop in the grass of the lawn as he turned in the direction of the highway. Hannah watched until he disappeared from sight over the rise of the hill. She turned to see Fergus heading around the house, sniffing as he went.

"Come on," she said to Teagan. "Let's get our swimsuits and head out."

While Teagan was organizing her swim bag, Hannah sent Jackie a text to let her know to expect them. She also sent a text to Oscar at the museum to check in on the status of the situation. She knew the news crew would have made their way there by now. With the director out of the office there was no one on hand to cope with whatever popped up. She felt a niggle of guilt then firmly closed her mind to such thoughts. Let the investigative team deal with the press. They worked for the state parks system, too, and they were calling the shots. Let them take all the flack.

It occurred to her that the director hadn't told her he was going to be out of the office. Where was he, she wondered.

* * *

Scoop had climbed down to the body. It rested precariously on a small ledge. It was going to be difficult to get it back up to the lookout point of Dowdell's Knob. Each footfall sent a small cascade of pebbles tumbling down. One false move would send the body careening down the mountain.

He used his cell phone on the climb down, trying to capture as much evidence as he could. There wasn't much. Three people had made the descent and back up again since the discovery of the body, all of them in need of handholds and toeholds. Their tracks would make it impossible to place any significance on any broken foliage or disturbed rock or soil.

He looked up from his perch beside the body. The odd formation of the protrusion that had hidden it from view was a problem. How had it come to rest in this spot? Surely the overhanging boulder would have deflected it out and into the valley below.

The immediate area was scuffed up with footprints. He took a close-up photo of the different shoe patterns but they had crisscrossed each other to the point that there wasn't a full print he could capture for comparison.

Teagan's words about the odd positioning of D'Amboise's body came back to him. The resting place beneath the overhang was troublesome. Something about it was wrong. It was possible he slid further down the trail after impact, Scoop supposed. The laws of physics and all that.

It was imperative they identify the man as soon as possible. Only then could they begin the process of eliminating him from any connection with D'Amboise. Curtis Arthur D'Amboise. Why had he really been in Warm Springs?

Callahan sat on the rock formation looking down at him and the dead man. Scoop didn't have the energy to be annoyed. He studied the placement of the corpse. The only way to get to the lower portion of the trail was to climb back up and over the protrusion of rock. As he did so, he saw where the second official on the scene had climbed that route before him. They would get nothing further from the scene.

Chapter Eleven

*O*n the surface it appears a hiker has taken a fatal tumble over the edge of the lookout point at Dowdell's Knob. It happens.

But to have two deaths in this sleepy southwest corner of Georgia, both in the parks so closely associated with Roosevelt, and both within twenty-four hours makes the fur on the back of my neck stand up. The deaths seem unrelated. One is murder. The other has all the appearances of an accident. Coincidence? I don't like coincidences and neither, apparently, does Scoop. He has taken on that introspective gaze-into-the-distance stance I've come to recognize.

Wisely, he's taking the necessary precautions with the scene that I would if I had opposable thumbs. And an iPhone. Documentation is crucial. Evidence has already been lost by the efforts of the local cops but that can't be helped. We must proceed with the cards we're dealt.

And speaking of a good hand, Scoop looks up and gives a wave.

Birdie is peering over the rim. That means McFadden can't be far behind.

Scoop starts the climb back to the lookout point. I think I'll take advantage of the opportunity to scout about on my own. Of my many talents, a keen eye has served me well over the years. I confess that my equally keen sense of smell is, at the moment, overwhelmed by the deteriorating corpse.

Our dead hiker doesn't look the part. Shorts are not a good look for him. Talk about being blinded by the white! Slide-on sneakers aren't exactly the proper footwear for scrambling down a mountain goat path on the side of a ravine either. If, in fact, our dead man was a hiker he clearly didn't arrive at this spot with the intention of actually hiking.

He's accustomed to being in the sun, so there's that on the outdoorsy side of things. His arms, face, and neck are nicely tanned. He also knew to wear a hat as his bald pate is nearly as white as his legs. I suspect hiking isn't really his thing, that he might be exactly what he appears to be, a tourist who wandered too close to danger.

* * *

"I haven't moved the body to check for ID. He's perched in a difficult spot. I didn't want to risk sending him into a slide down the mountain." Scoop dusted his hands together then wiped sweat from his brow. "The Pine Mountain chief has a harness and ropes. It'll take a two-man team but I'd like Mac to get some shots first."

McFadden watched the local patrol officer checking the climbing gear. "Right, Boss." He took a camera from the case at his feet and added a lead line to it. He clipped the other end of the line to his belt.

"A hiker?" Birdie asked.

Scoop frowned and gave a small shake of his head.

"Not sure. He's not equipped for it."

"Tourist, then. Poor devil."

Scoop made no reply. Instead, he looked down the lane at the picnic area where the hiker who discovered the body was sitting. He had his head down on his folded arms.

"Talk to the responding officer. I'll get a statement from the kid."

Scoop felt the drop in temperature as soon as he walked under the shade of the trees overhanging the lane leading toward the highway. The picnic tables were situated in a pleasant setting to enjoy the tranquility of the spot. It was no wonder FDR loved it here.

That was the thing, wasn't it? This accident hadn't happened at any number of scenic spots around Pine Mountain but rather here, in a favorite spot of the thirty-second president. He couldn't ignore the potential link until the body was identified and his reason for being on the mountain determined.

As Scoop approached the witness, he cleared his throat. The hiker lifted his head.

"You up to answering some questions?"

He nodded.

"Your name's Larry, right?"

"Larry Hightower."

"How did you get up here?"

"Hiked from The Country Kitchen. Had lunch there. Charged my phone."

"Headed where?"

"Well, here. Then on to Warm Springs. Wanted to see the pools."

"Ever been here before?"

Larry shook his head.

"Do a lot of hiking?"

"In the Carolinas mostly. And California some."

"Both coasts." Scoop took a seat across the table from him. "Any particular reason for that?"

"School. Duke and UCLA."

"Did you see anyone in the area when you arrived?"

He shook his head. "The gray SUV was here."

"What about the other car? The white one?"

"That's the search and rescue guy's car. He was the first one here. I guess they have to see for themselves that he's dead. Then the patrol car arrived."

Scoop thought for a moment. "What about on the highway? Any other hikers? Was there much traffic?"

"Two people on bikes passed me but they were headed in this direction, not away." He shrugged. "Not much traffic." He had been focused on his clasped hands throughout the interview. He lifted his gaze. "One had a government tag."

"Driving in the direction you were walking?"

"No. He was coming toward me."

"How did you know it had a government tag if it was going south?"

"I turned to look. He was flying around the curve. Going way too fast."

"Did you get the number?"

Larry shook his head. "It surprised me is all. I didn't think to get the number."

"Where can I reach you if I have more questions?"

"I hadn't made any real plans. I just came down to do the Pine Mountain range and see the FDR park and sites. Just passing time until I head to Boston and a new job."

"Graduated college?"

He nodded.

"You look awfully young."

He shrugged.

Scoop noted his cell phone number and home address in his notebook. When Larry declined a ride to Warm Springs, Scoop told him to keep his cell phone charged and headed back to the recovery scene.

* * *

Hannah and Teagan found Sue lounging by the pool at the Lodge at the Calloway Gardens resort. She was in a recliner under an umbrella with a wrap over her swimsuit and a book open on the table beside her. She waved when she saw them approaching.

"Where's everyone?" Hannah asked as she pulled a recliner close enough to share the shade of the umbrella.

"Jackie's on her laptop taking care of a few emails. Apparently, it's impossible for a website builder to really take time off. And Phyllis is shopping."

"Her favorite pastime," Sue and Hannah said in unison.

They laughed.

"Hey, Teagan, that's a smart looking swimsuit." Sue gave her nose a gentle tweak.

"Thanks." Teagan smiled. She appeared more relaxed than she had been on the previous evening around the friends.

Hannah rubbed sunscreen on Teagan's face and shoulders. "There you go, Bean. Go cool off in the pool."

Teagan walked to the edge of the deep end of the pool and executed a neat dive into the water. The two sorority sisters watched her for a while.

"Tell me what's going on," Sue said.

"The media. A station out of Atlanta sent a news van. They've been to the museum asking questions. It's only a matter of time."

"Maybe they won't make the connection."

Hannah watched Teagan cutting through the pool with smooth, swift strokes. "Maybe."

"So, what's the plan? Teagan could stay here at the Lodge with us. A real slumber party weekend."

Hannah thought about the suggestion for a few minutes. It would keep Teagan out of the scorching eye of the reporters. And it would take her out of the heart of the investigation. But for how long? "I don't know. She worries about me." She looked over at Sue. "Crazy, right? She's only ten. But there it is. I guess I didn't handle things very well when David died. I should have kept myself under better control through all of it."

"It's not your fault. The circumstances of his death were horrible enough. The relentless hounding by the press was uncalled for and I don't think anyone could have gotten through that unscathed."

Hannah gave her friend a weak smile and laid her head against the backrest of the lounger. She closed her eyes and tried to relax. Last night had been pretty much sleepless. She had been afraid to fall into a deep sleep. Afraid of the images that would come, as they always did, when she was stressed. Those images flashed through her mind now. The news coverage on national television of David, bound and gagged, on his knees, flanked by the dark-robed terrorists.

Her eyes flew open and she sat up straighter, her gaze sweeping the pool for Teagan. Fergus placed his head on her knee, his eyes intent on her face. Hannah absently scratched behind his ears. Teagan had joined a game with some kids in the pool seeing who could stay under water the longest. The sing-song counting of the children reminding her to relax, breathe, let go of the memories.

Chapter Twelve

It's beautiful here. I can understand why FDR chose this spot for his picnic parties. And why hikers walk these trails. They do require a bit of stamina and sure feet. No problem for the likes of me but I have my doubts about our latest victim.

My senses are tingling. It's the position of the body. I found nothing useful on the ledge. Too many people have left a mess of things. There are traces of blood leading down from the top. As the police officer said, troublesome.

The Pine Mountain police chief found no identification on the victim. In fact, his pockets were completely empty. No wallet, no keys, no cell phone. There's no sign of the compulsory items people find so essential. Yet, a car is here. With what I have learned are New York license plates. Which is somewhere North of Warm Springs, apparently. Interesting.

I think it would be prudent to explore the terrain below the trail. If this is no accident, and I suspect it isn't, the surest way to dispose of anything that could identify the victim is to give it a good toss down the mountainside.

The law can search their database for information but, in my humble opinion, hard physical evidence trumps computer printouts. Besides, nothing pieces together a crime scene like good old-fashioned paws-on-the-ground. Especially since my paws are so very nimble.

I look up at the rim at Dowdell's Knob and assess the potential trajectory of various objects. A cell phone or keys would fly pretty far out if the pitcher had a good arm. Sunglasses or a wallet, a bit less. All that makes for a lot of terrain to cover so I'd better hustle.

* * *

The police chief of Pine Mountain handed Scoop a sheet of notebook paper. On it was the NY license plate number and a name and address.

"Stella Abromowitz. New York City address. That's the owner of the car. Forty-seven years old."

Scoop read the note. "Anyone try to reach her?"

"No answer on the home line. They're sending a patrol car around to check the apartment."

"What about locally? She could be staying at Callaway Gardens or another hotel."

"I've got my dispatcher making calls. One of my men is checking property ownership to see if she owns a house or condo in the area. But she could be visiting friends or staying in a rental."

Or her body could be further down the mountain, Scoop thought.

The police chief's brow furrowed more deeply. "It's getting late in the day. Not much we can accomplish here once the light gets behind the ridge. We need to make sure Mrs. Abromowitz is accounted for. If she isn't, that's a whole other can of worms."

"Agreed." Scoop fell silent for a moment. Finally, he said, "I don't have a good feeling about this. Let's see if she has a neighbor, relative, someone who knows where she might be. I assume you've done a cell phone search."

"Yep."

"And?"

"Goes straight to voice mail."

"See if they can locate the signal. Let me know if you have any luck. We need to identify our victim and see if there's any connection between the two. My guess would be yes."

"Agreed."

Scoop turned from the lip of the drop-off. "Alert the FBI in Atlanta that we might need the use of cadaver dogs first thing tomorrow. And a helicopter." Their presence would be warranted if they were looking for another victim.

The body from the ledge had been loaded into an ambulance. It would go straight to the coroner's office in Columbus. Scoop felt pretty sure the autopsy would support the growing suspicion in his gut. Whoever he was, he had died of blunt force trauma and from what he could discover from the scene, it wasn't due to an accidental fall.

So, what was his next move? He watched the ambulance pull away. Birdie and McFadden had roped off the lookout point and were loading up their gear.

Scoop caught the police chief as he was getting into his car. "You have someone you can post here tonight?"

"You think that's necessary?"

"At the moment, yes."

The chief hesitated, then nodded. "I'll split the shift between a couple of my men."

With that reassurance, Scoop got into his car and headed to Warm Springs and the incident room at the police station.

* * *

The three sorority sisters were sharing a suite at the Lodge. Jackie came out of her room when Sue, Hannah, and Teagan came up from the pool.

"How was the water?" she asked Teagan.

"Fine."

"It was a short swim."

"There was a man talking to Mom."

Jackie looked to Hannah as Sue chimed in. "He was an old slimeball trying to flirt with Hannah."

Teagan giggled at Sue's description of the interloper. Then the smile faded and she said, "I think he was a reporter."

"Is that a bad thing?"

Teagan looked to her mother. "I don't know."

Hannah took the towel around Teagan's shoulders and vigorously dried her hair. "He was a Nosy Parker and I don't want to be drawn into the gossip about the death at the museum."

"Who's hungry?" Jackie asked. "I just ordered up a fruit and cheese platter but I think we need to add some sandwiches to the order."

Teagan's expression brightened. "Or pizza?"

"Pizza it is," Jackie replied.

During this exchange, Fergus had made a thorough inspection of the suite. He couldn't find a spot where he wanted to settle.

Teagan went to his side as he looked around anxiously. "What's wrong, Fergus?"

Hannah went to sit on the floor beside Teagan and the Scottie. "I think he's feeling a little outnumbered. This is his first outing with The Girls."

On cue, the sorority sisters all giggled and piled into the huddle with Fergus at the center. They hugged, kissed, and tickled the dog and Teagan until they were all squealing with laughter.

Phyllis arrived at that moment heavily laden with shopping bags. "What's this? A slumber party in full force without me?" She dropped her packages onto the sofa and joined in the fun until a knock on the door had them untangling themselves for their room service delivery.

After the feast, Teagan went to Phyllis's bathroom to shower.

Hannah watched Fergus sitting in front of the door to Phyllis's bedroom. He monitored Teagan's every move. Nothing would happen to her on his watch. If only he could protect them from the scrutiny of a full-blown news story. They would have to be very careful. If anyone recognized her, the focus would shift and their lives would be a living nightmare. Again.

Chapter Thirteen

It's hot enough to dry chili peppers here on this side of the mountain. I could enjoy a nice drink of cool water right about now. I've covered a lot of ground but the truth is, there's way too much hillside for one cat to search. It's like looking for a needle in a haystack.

Besides, it's getting late and I've worked up an appetite. Better make my way topside. This little bit of a trail will do nicely. Probably made by the local animal population. There're snatches of fur caught in the encroaching brambles. And that's a snake skin for sure.

But what's this?

This pelt belongs to no animal I know of. Just look at the size of it. And it isn't even fur!

Scoop needs to see this. Should I move it from this spot? I think I'll have to. I'm afraid it will be too difficult to convince him to follow me down the mountain. His hardheadedness is becoming a major roadblock to our investigation.

I judge the distance to the rim to be about forty yards. This thistle makes a good marker for Birdie or McFadden to return to the scene. Hopefully one of them will prove more reasonable about following my lead.

This thing is nasty and reeks of sweat. Gross! It's enough to make a cat gag. Regardless, this is the only way to get it up the mountain. My taste buds will never be the same and I do love a good chow down. Why I should care about the ways of men, I don't know. The things I do to get to the answer to a puzzle! Curiosity. It will be the end of me.

The last five yards are the worst. Not only are the pads of my paws scratched and blistered, but this mangy thing has made my thirst worse.

Finally, I top the rim to find … no one.

* * *

Scoop read through the file Clay Bishop had downloaded on Curtis Arthur D'Amboise. He had three known aliases and had fled Sarasota, Florida, ahead of a fraud investigation. A horse trainer was questioning the pedigree of a race horse the dead man had sold to a wealthy owner of one of the more prestigious stables in the area.

In Dallas, Texas, he had passed himself off as a real estate developer for Bill Gates researching sites for a research and development center in a more tax friendly state.

An older investigation in New Jersey had something to do with passing off fake precious stones to an upscale jeweler.

Curtis Arthur D'Amboise was beginning to resemble his initials. Now to discover what scam he was running in

Warm Springs.

Scoop was thankful for the interagency co-operation between both local police departments and the state parks' arm of law enforcement. Still, with a murder scene in one jurisdiction and a suspicious death in another, his support team was pushed to the limit. He had already called in a four-man search team to help scour the terrain of the museum grounds for the murder scene. Even with the help of the local police and volunteers, they had turned up nothing useful. With the Abromowitz woman unaccounted for, the case could easily spread to the federal level. Two bodies were bad enough. He prayed there wouldn't be a third.

The two deaths were connected, Scoop was sure of that. It was too great a coincidence otherwise. He felt the pressure to discover the identity of their latest corpse and why he was in the area. If he was staying locally, they needed to determine where. Scoop suspected this was Alice's wayward hotel guest. The time frame fit. He needed to get an ID but there was no way he could show her the photos of the dead man. They would have to wait for the coroner to give them a name. Assuming, of course, that a fingerprint was obtainable.

There wasn't anything further he could do until something popped.

"I'm headed back to the B&B. D'Amboise's room deserves another look." Scoop closed the D'Amboise file and stood.

"We searched it thoroughly, Boss," Birdie said.

"I know. Just a feeling I'm missing something. You and Mac should get some dinner. The Bulloch House is pretty good."

"Will do, Boss."

Scoop left his car parked at the police station and

crossed Broad Street to walk along the raised sidewalk past the shops to the B&B. As on the previous day, the reception was empty as was the ice cream shop.

He mounted the stairs to the third floor. All was quiet. The hallway was dim, with the only illumination coming from the dining area. As he made his way toward the door to D'Amboise's room, he took the key from his pocket. As he fitted it into the lock, a faint sound caused him to turn just as something hard and heavy cracked him on the head. He went out like a light.

* * *

By the time Hannah and Teagan left the Lodge at Callaway Gardens, Teagan seemed relaxed and happy. The pizza party had been a great success and a lively game of Monopoly had left her in possession of all the high rent properties. The most telling behavior was that she placed Fergus in the back seat where he normally rode as they piled into the car for the trip home.

Hannah hadn't given in to the desire to dial Scoop's number until late. After vacillating throughout the course of the afternoon, she finally decided she needed to know the status of the investigation and whether or not the museum would be allowed to open the following day. The likelihood was remote but it was a legitimate reason to reach out to him, she decided. One that wouldn't seem as if she were pursuing him. Which she wasn't. Definitely not.

Her call had gone unanswered. She tried not to read anything into that. He was investigating a murder, after all. And there was the complication of the news media crawling all over the place. No doubt he had his hands full.

The sing of the tires on the highway lulled her into thoughts of their days at college, the excitement of being an adult, on her own for the first time in her life, searching for her true identity. It had been a delicious, heady rush of possibilities. There had been no one to tell her what time to be in at night, who was or wasn't suitable to date, to keep her head out of the clouds and on her education. And then there had been Scoop.

If she was being honest with herself, she felt the attraction now. Maybe not the same mad rush of hormones and lost appetite, but a slow pull that turned her thoughts to him in the oddest moments.

A car passed her as she came out of one of the corkscrew curves coming down the mountain and roared ahead. It jolted her back to the moment. She realized, as it sped away down the highway that it was a law enforcement car, whether the Pine Mountain police or Warm Springs, she couldn't say. She chastised herself for daydreaming about things that weren't meant to be and focused on the road ahead. After a sleepless night and a stressful day, she was ready for her bed.

The warm glow of lights on the carport were welcoming and reassuring. She really should thank Billy Brad properly for his kindness. Maybe some fudge squares from the Tuscawilla Ice Cream Parlor. Fergus had no complaints as they piled out of the car. The kitchen door was firmly locked as she had left it and Hannah felt no qualms as they stepped inside. At last, all was right with her world. For the moment, anyway.

The bedtime ritual was soon accomplished and Teagan fell to sleep quickly. Hannah peeped into her room one last time to find Fergus on guard at her bedside. She left the door ajar. Even as she chided herself, she couldn't resist one last look at her phone as she plugged it into the charger. There were no messages, no texts. Had Scoop misread her intentions with her call? She frowned and turned resolutely from the phone. As she snuggled between the sheets, she vowed to put him out of her mind. Though it was early, she was bone tired. She needed a good night's sleep.

Chapter Fourteen

Well, this is a fine how do you do. Here I sit with my hard-won find, a dusty, briar entangled mess. The whole area is quiet, empty. Not even a passing vehicle on the highway some hundred or so yards away can be heard.

What to do?

Ah, what's this I see? Headlights are winking through the trees as a car approaches, headed straight to the lookout point of Dowdell's Knob. I believe the cavalry has arrived. And a good thing, too, because I'm parched, tired, and hungry. One of those catfish filets at the Bulloch House would be just the thing. I would even settle for Trudy the Tour Guide's tuna salad right about now.

The car rolls to a stop almost at my feet. It has the drawings of officialdom on the door. A young man steps out and gazes at the star-filled night making a spectacular sky above the valley before us.

Which is all very well and good, but I'm in need of help.

Abruptly he turns back toward the patrol car and in so doing, sees me.

"Well, well," *he says.* "How did you get way out here?"

He reaches down to pet me. I allow this familiarity since I need his help. Finally, he picks me up, completely ignoring the nasty, tangled pelt.

I squirm and twist and execute a perfect four-point landing and take a stance beside the smelly tangle.

"Not used to people, hey?"

We do a stare-down.

"You don't look feral." *He puts his hands in his pockets and sways back onto his heels.* "Your owner dumped you? Is that it?"

Seriously? It has been a hard day and now I have to do the mime bit to get my point across. It's times like this that I begin to wonder why I try.

And just like that, the patrolman toes the nasty clump at his feet.

"What's this?" *he asks.*

Now we're getting somewhere.

"You caught yourself a muskrat for supper?"

I sit back on my haunches and simply stare. Sometimes there's just no light in the attic.

"You hungry, are you?"

He studies me a moment. "Thirsty, too, I'd bet."

Well, now, maybe I was a bit hasty in my assessment. That can happen. Granted, it doesn't happen often, but still, I could be wrong about Bubba. He's definitely showing signs of intelligence.

"You look all done in." *Bubba studies me a moment.*

Okay, I admit I've been harsh in my judgment. But in my defense, it's been a hard day's work on the mountainside.

Bubba opens the car door and rummages around a bit. He emerges with a bottle of water and what looks like the aluminum tin of one of those snack size pecan pies. He pours water into it for me.

I look up at my newfound friend in gratitude before I quickly lap up the refreshing water and watch as he refills the container. Yes, a true friend, indeed.

"What I can't figure," *Bubba says,* "is how the dickens you got way out here."

Naturally, I have no explanation so we settle into companionable silence and watch the night sky.

"It's peaceful out here at night. I guess when you live here all the time you forget to look up and see all this glory."

Bubba falls silent as we contemplate the universe.

"I can see why the President loved it up here. Wonder if he ever came here at night to see this sky?" *He nods to himself.* "I'm sure he did."

Bubba once again rummages around in the police vehicle and comes out with a tin of something in his hand. The moment he pulls the tab on the quite inventive container, the tantalizing aroma of fish fills the air and my mouth waters in anticipation.

Mackerel in mustard sauce is one of life's finer experiences. Seriously. And Bubba is quite generous. He has forever cemented our friendship.

We both sigh with contentment and as he leans against the hood of the vehicle, he again toes the matted, nasty clump. After a moment, he squats beside it, takes a pen from his shirt pocket and uses it to move the odious object about.

Abruptly he stands. "I think what we have here is a two-pay."

I've never encountered a two-pay before so I hop down from the hood of the car and look closely at the clump.

"The dead man wore a rug!"

* * *

Scoop grunted at the sharp pain that flashed at his temples as he rolled over. He opened his eyes to the dim light of a small space with a door on one wall and a set of stairs leading down opposite it. He sat up and the room began to spin. When that passed, he felt the back of his head. His fingers came away bloody. After a mental rundown of his other body parts, he leveraged his weight against a wall and stood. Everything seemed to be working.

The door was locked. He rattled the doorknob but it wouldn't budge. The light in the small space came from the well of the stairs. Scoop gripped the banister against a wave of dizziness and slowly began to descend.

At the foot of the stairs a door opened onto the parking lot at the side of the bed and breakfast. A street light illuminated the Dollar General store across the railroad track. The traffic light at the intersection turned from red to green. Scoop stood on the narrow porch and checked his surroundings. The small gardening oasis lay in shadow. Three cars were in the semi-darkness of the parking lot.

He went back into the hotel, past the staircase, through a room, then a hallway that led to a door. When he turned the handle, it opened into the reception area. Alice looked up from a laptop that she was pecking away at as the door opened.

"Good, Lord!" She hurried to Scoop's side. "Whatever happened to you?"

"Has anyone been down the stairs in the last few minutes?"

Alice guided him to a chair and made him sit down. She peered at the wound on the back of his head then glanced at the clock on the wall behind reception. "No one's been in or out in the last fifteen minutes. I came in from folding laundry in the back of the hotel at a few minutes before eight."

Scoop did the math. He'd been out a good fifteen minutes. His head was throbbing in earnest now. He tried to stand.

Alice firmly pushed him back into the chair. "We'll have none of that. This wound needs seeing to." She crossed the foyer to the ice cream shop and returned with a cloth filled with ice which she placed gingerly on his head. "Hold it there while I call Doc."

Scoop let Alice hold sway in the matter and set his mind to the problem of who had cracked him on the head. He'd seen no one when he entered the hotel and there had been the quiet of abandonment about the old building. Someone had been lying in wait.

He searched his pockets for his phone and found it was missing. So, too, was his notebook. Somewhere in the investigation he had stumbled onto something the killer didn't want him to know. Why else would he take the notebook?

At that moment, Birdie entered the hotel. "Jeez, Boss. What happened?"

Scoop glanced at Alice who was behind the registration desk on the phone with the doctor. "Ambushed outside the victim's room. He took my phone and notebook."

"Did you get a look at him?" Birdie lifted the makeshift ice pack and winced.

"No. Struck from behind. I think whoever it was wanted to get into D'Amboise's room. Go check it out. There's something we've missed."

* * *

Hannah woke with a start. She lay quietly listening. Nothing stirred in the little farmhouse. What had awakened her?

She got quietly out of the bed and, without turning on a light, padded toward the kitchen on bare feet. Fergus lifted his head as she peeped into Teagan's room but then rested his chin on his paws and closed his eyes.

In the kitchen, Hannah filled a glass with water and drank it as she stood looking out the window at the night sky. The shadows around the lone oak tree in the corner of the yard were ink black. Nothing stirred on the landscape. Yet she felt a sense of unease.

Something teased at the edge of her mind. Something that had obviously surfaced in her subconscious while she slept. Whatever it was, it continued to escape her grasp.

Chapter Fifteen

My new friend spent a few minutes on the walkie-talkie in his patrol car speaking in a strange code. Within a very short time another patrol car arrived at Dowdell's Knob with the Pine Mountain Chief of Police. There was a conversation about me, the two-pay, and what the heck I was doing on the mountain in the first place.

Finally, the two-pay was placed in a bag and I was unceremoniously dropped onto the back seat of the chief's car. A short ride, equally as hair-raising as the one with Scoop, soon had us back down the mountain and in the Warm Springs police station. McFadden pulled on plastic gloves and examined the smelly rug. When he was finished, he booted up his laptop and clicked the little thing called a mouse a number of times. Finally, he stopped on an image that filled the computer screen. It's the photo of a man. And I know him.

McFadden keeps clicking the little mouse. The photo changes to an array of two-pays that resemble the one I found on the mountainside, only free of debris and combed. He then selects one of these and with a click of the mouse it suddenly rests on the head of the dead man from Dowdell's Knob. After trying, then discarding several of the rugs, he's satisfied with the image.

Well, well, you learn something new every day. A two-pay is fake hair. Why anyone would wear such a thing on their head in the Georgia heat is beyond me but, as I've said before, humans don't always act in their own best interest.

"Bingo," *McFadden says.* "I do believe we've found the missing guest from the bed and breakfast. This should help to discover who he is. The coroner already has the body. Let's hope he can find a usable print and give us a quick ID."

McFadden grinned and chucked me under the chin. "Good work, Callahan. You're turning into quite the detective. Dirty Harry has nothing on you."

I don't know who this Dirty Harry is but everyone seems to know him. And, if I understand the hint of admiration from both Dax and McFadden when they speak of him, he's someone they look up to.

I'll take that as a good thing.

* * *

Scoop conceded to sitting in a chair in the doorway to D'Amboise's room while the doctor put three quick stitches in his scalp. His head hurt like a son-of-a-gun but he declined anything for the pain. He was now officially ticked-off. Whoever was behind the death of D'Amboise had escalated the stakes.

He watched Birdie as she felt up the length of each panel of the drapes at the window, along the hem, and across the top of the window sill. Painstakingly she made her way all around the perimeter of the room. She checked the drain of the sink and along the pipe where it abutted the wall.

The doctor dabbed the stitches with cotton gauze doused in something that stung, then proclaimed he had done all he could do, and that Scoop really should have his head examined. With a sigh he packed up his bag and left in the face of Scoop's grunted reply.

As soon as the doctor turned the corner to descend the stairs, Scoop went to the head of the bed. He grabbed the iron headboard and pulled it away from the wall.

"You shouldn't be doing that!" Birdie complained as she grabbed the other side of the bed and pulled.

They found nothing taped to the wall, stuffed between the mattresses, or hidden in the bedding.

Scoop sighed. He had been sure the cat was after something hidden behind the bed. He stood there a moment, staring without seeing the intricate pattern of the oriental carpet, trying to decide on his next step. Suddenly he focused and with the toe of his shoe flipped back the carpet.

There, a good six inches from the edge, was an SD card.

"Well, well," said Birdie, "what have we here?"

Scoop bent down and picked up the small, flat, storage device. "Five gets you ten it's motive."

* * *

Hannah tried to settle into sleep but it wouldn't come.

She realized that they had gone to bed way too early. The initial exhaustion she'd felt upon arriving home from Callaway had allowed her to quickly drop off to sleep but now she was wide awake.

She got out of bed and made a circuit of the house, checking the windows and doors by touch. Everything was secure. Try as she might, she couldn't call up the subconscious thought that had awakened her. It would come to her, she decided, if she stopped trying to recapture it.

With a sigh, she turned on the bedroom lamp and pulled her laptop from the bedside table thinking the boredom of working her way through work emails would solve her sleeplessness.

Fergus came to peer at her through the open door and she softly shooed him away.

It was amazing how quickly her inbox had filled in a single day. As she began to scan the emails, she sat up straighter in bed. There were dozens from unfamiliar addresses. As she clicked on first one then another, she realized they were all about the dead body at the museum.

It seemed every online news site on the web wanted a quote about what had happened. The questions ranged from cause of death, to whether she had personally seen the body, to had there been a lot of blood.

This was bad. It was really bad. This meant that the media circus was warming up for a full out campaign.

After the first few emails, Hannah began deleting them without reading their content. Until she came to a name that seemed familiar. She clicked on it and read the message.

I know who you are.

Chapter Sixteen

I confess, being the hero of the hour isn't a bad gig. Everyone seems to think I'm some kind of cat genius. Which, of course, isn't far from the truth.

Except for Clay.

"He's just a cat! Probably thought it was something to eat or something."

I shudder at the thought but, then, I haven't been overly impressed with Clay's skills at deduction though I'm sure he's a very good patrolman.

McFadden's phone pings and he checks his messages. "Winner, winner, chicken dinner. Our dead hiker is one Anthony Rousso. I'm sharing the file to your computer now."

Billy Brad logs into his computer and a photo of Anthony Rousso fills the screen. In his mug shot he isn't wearing the rug.

McFadden's phone chirps again. He moves away from the officers gathered around Billy Brad's computer screen. "Yeah, Birdie."

He listens to a one-sided conversation. "Sure thing," *he concludes.* "I'm on my way."

"Take That Darn Cat with you," *says Clay as McFadden packs up one of his cases.*

There's no need for McFadden to take me anywhere for I've had quite enough excitement for one day. All the hoopla that comes with dead bodies is exhausting. And, Clay's attitude about my contribution to the case aside, searching the mountainside is hot, hard work. I think I'll do a short version of my usual reconnaissance about the town and find a quiet porch swing to settle in for the night.

Our little rural town closes up early. The last of the kitchen help are leaving The Bulloch House. All the little shops are closed for the day. It must be getting on toward ten o'clock. I hear the distant rumble of a train that has passed through in the last few minutes and I head in the direction of the tracks. The little farmhouse of the Lately Departed Rooster is just along the way and The Wife makes bacon and eggs early every morning. The glider on the front porch has a nice soft cushion. Yes, a good night's rest and I'll be myself again.

As I make my way along the tracks, I see a glow in the distance. I smell the wood smoke. There, in a little clearing near The Farmer's garden is Dax, sitting before a campfire with a tent nearby. He looks up from the flames as I draw near.

"Well," *he says,* "I thought I'd seen the last of you."

I go and sit near him but well out of the way of the fire. I hear the blast of the train in the far distance as it approaches a crossing somewhere in the countryside. If not for the murder at the museum, Dax would be long gone from Warm Springs. A man on the move, a man of adventure. It has a certain appeal.

"I thought about hopping the train." *Dax sighs.* "It would only mean trouble. Someone would probably drag me back because they can't figure out who the murderer is." *He looks at me, grins, and shakes his head.* "It's not me, boss, but no one's listening to me so I guess I'll have to wait it out."

It seems Dax is lonely. I suppose that's to be expected of someone who's a wanderer. Unlike cats, humans aren't meant to be alone. Though I am bone tired, I decide to keep him company for a while.

He sighs again. "Should have left a day earlier." *He throws a small twig onto the blaze and it sparks brightly for a brief moment.* "Just my luck they'd find the body on the day I decide to visit the museum. It's a worrisome business. Don't like being caught up in stuff not of my doing."

Well, who does? Oh. Me. Right. But that's because I'm curious. It's my weakness. I confess, I can't resist a good puzzle and a murder is the best puzzle of all. I'm quite determined to solve it.

Dax moves a tin plate closer to me. I see it contains a bit of blueberry cobbler. The Farmer's Wife makes a tasty blueberry cobbler.

Dax watches me eat. He rubs my back, smoothing my fur until I begin to purr. We sit that way a while, then he banks the campfire and crawls into the low, small, tent, leaving the flap open. He shifts about a bit then is totally still. Within minutes I hear a gentle snore. I think of the soft cushion on the glider on The Farmer's porch. Then I move into the tent and settle at Dax's feet.

✳ ✳ ✳

McFadden inserted the SD card into one of his cameras and clicked play. D'Amboise had recorded short snippets of footage of Warm Springs, the memorabilia on display in the hotel lobby, and numerous items in the museum. He had also recorded a pretty waitress singing as she served him his lunch. D'Amboise could be heard on the recording as he flirted with her. He had a deep, velvety voice and he had a way with words. The singing waitress would be the no-show from the Bulloch House earlier in the day, Scoop decided. She had a good voice, too.

Of more particular interest to Scoop and his team were several attempts on the part of D'Amboise to waylay the guest Alice had referred to as "posh." He asked her questions about the Roosevelts. She remained unflustered by his gambits and managed to sidestep him or verbally outmaneuver him on each attempt until the fourth time.

There, on the video, Scoop and his team saw Joyce Favor as she attempted to leave The Bulloch House by the side entrance. They had no doubt the exit route was to avoid D'Amboise but he was close on her heels. He had the camera up and recording when suddenly the image jumped wildly up to a view of the sky then tumbled to the brick pavers. In so doing, it caught the desert boots and army camouflage of a pair of pants before going dark.

"Do we know where he is?" Scoop asked.

McFadden shook his head. "Should we alert the Warm Springs police?"

Scoop thought for a moment. "Not yet. He can't know we're on to him. He'll probably be at the restaurant tomorrow. He'll know they can use him until he's free to leave town. Plus, it gives him cover and food for the time being. Even a hobo has to eat. We can grab him up nice and quiet when we're ready."

"But what if he decides to run?" Birdie looked anxiously at the gash on Scoop's head. "He knows he's stepped in it with the attack on you. And he didn't get what he was looking for."

"If that's the case, he'll already have left the area."

"I don't like it," McFadden said. "He'll be long gone by morning."

"Maybe. But he's got no transportation. It won't be hard to track him down."

"So why not grab him up now?"

"Whoever hit me took my notebook."

"So?"

"Why?"

McFadden shrugged. "To see if we had already found the evidence. To find out what we know."

"How does that help him? If we had found the evidence, he would already be in custody. If we keep things quiet for now, he'll think we didn't find it. That's his mission right now. To find and destroy the evidence. That's when he'll show his hand. Nothing else links him to the victim."

"We have two victims, Boss." Birdie said.

"Yes. We do. And we need to know how they're connected if we're ever going to find the motive."

McFadden cleared his throat. "We have an ID, Boss. Should have mentioned it straight away."

"That was quick."

"Because of the news coverage of the D'Amboise death, the coroner came into the morgue as soon as they got the body to Columbus. As deteriorated as it was, he was able to get a good enough thumb print. He was in the database." McFadden opened his laptop and brought up the file. "He was one Anthony Rousso, a former middle weight boxer, club bouncer, and bail bondsman from Boca Raton.

"That's two bodies. Both men from Florida. What are the odds?"

"I'd take that bet."

"Me too," Scoop said. "Me too. Now let's find the connection."

* * *

Hannah stared at the email message; her heart frozen in her chest.

We need to talk.

And soon.

It was from Chase Gibbons, the reporter with *The LaGrange Daily News* who had called the museum office earlier. There was a thinly veiled threat in his wording.

David's capture by a terrorist group emulating the Taliban had received coverage worldwide. The threat had been that he would meet the same fate as other captives and that it would be telecast live unless several million dollars in ransom were delivered to the group. In the end, David had died during the military's effort to extract him from the enemy stronghold.

The news coverage during and after the debacle had sent Hannah and Teagan into hiding. And now that Teagan was regaining a sense of normalcy in her life, this reporter was threatening to stir it all up again.

She couldn't let that happen.

Meet me in the butterfly garden at Callaway tomorrow. Noon. Her finger hovered over the computer key for a brief hesitation, then she tapped send.

Chapter Seventeen

To awaken to the smell of bacon frying is one of life's little pleasures. To know that The Wife will share it with me when The Farmer is off on some errand about the farm adds an additional lift to my spirits. Dax seems to be of a like mind. He goes about his morning toiletry at a spigot near the barn.

I take a leisurely stroll around the premises, taking note of the number of chickens in the chicken yard, keeping my distance from the pig pen, and coming full circle to the back door of the farm house as the sound of the tractor sputters to life.

Dax is hard on my heels and The Wife feeds us both and refills Dax's coffee cup as she outlines what she would like for him to do. I hope some of the berries he's been instructed to pick from the brambles along the fence line will end up in a nice pie for supper.

Being a cat, I'm not expected to earn my supper so I saunter off in the direction of the hotel to see what Scoop and his crew are planning for the day.

It's a good thing that The Farmer and his Wife are early risers and I am once again "on the job" as the hotel is a hive of activity when I arrive. Two patrol cars are parked in front of the hotel. Several citizens of Warm Springs are looking on from across the street near the coffee shop.

Billy Brad is poking around the little gardening shed in the back corner of the parking lot. His back is to me as I approach from the railroad tracks. Suddenly, he gives a sharp whistle. A young man, also in uniform, comes from the direction of the alley.

"What ya got?" he asks as he approaches the gardening shed.

Billy Brad holds up a cell phone. "I think this is what we're looking for."

* * *

After a quick dusting with powder, Mac determined the phone had been wiped clean of fingerprints. Scoop unlocked it and did a quick scroll through his messages and texts. He saw that Hannah Sanderson had tried to call him twice late the day before.

"Can you tell if anything was accessed?" Clay asked.

Scoop shook his head. "I doubt it. Whoever attacked me must have quickly realized it required a code and that's why we were able to find it. It was of no use to him."

"But he has your notebook."

"I don't imagine that will be of much use, either. I have my own code for taking notes."

"Don't we all?" Clay replied. "So, what do you want to do about the drifter?"

The cat suddenly jumped onto the hotel dining room table and looked from Clay to Scoop.

"I don't know. I have a report on my phone on him but, obviously, I haven't had the chance to read through it. I think we're safe to assume he'll stick around town for a while, maybe turn up at The Bulloch House to work the lunch crowd."

"Unless he's already done a runner."

"True." Scoop opened one of the messages on his phone and read it. He slipped the phone into his pocket. "The coroner has his reports ready. There's something he wants me to see. I think we need to have all the facts before we make an arrest. The media has their teeth in this and we don't want to make a mistake this early in the case."

"You're going to Columbus?"

"I'll be back by noon. In the meantime, we need to keep searching for the murder weapon. I'll send McFadden and Birdie back to the museum to coordinate things."

"So, you want me to just sit on my hands until you get back?"

"Keep at the interviews of the locals and keep an eye out for the drifter but give him leeway to go about his business. Something about this doesn't feel right."

"Because he's ex-Army?"

"It's not that. He just doesn't strike me as someone who would have a stake one way or the other in D'Amboise's con, whatever that was. He isn't likely to be vested in the outcome either way so why would he intervene?"

"Saw Ms. Favor as a damsel in distress?"

Scoop thought about that for a moment. "She seemed capable of handling herself. Has your office been able to track her down?"

"Left a message with her housekeeper. She's due home today."

"Where's home?"

"Connecticut."

"Hmmm. Did the maid say why she was in Warm Springs?"

"Said I should ask Ms. Favor."

"So we shall."

What Scoop didn't share with Clay Bishop was that he was convinced it was someone with intimate knowledge of the museum and its workings who had placed the body in the servants' quarters.

D'Amboise had been pestering Joyce Favor with questions about the Roosevelts. Why her? Why would he consider her, a tourist in town, a source of information? Or had it been a ploy to engage someone who was clearly a woman of substance? D'Amboise was, after all, a con man always on the lookout for his next mark.

Scoop conferred with McFadden and Birdie on the search parameters before heading for his car. They needed to find the murder weapon!

His phone chirped and he checked the message. "The FBI has arrived at the scene on Dowdell's Knob. No one has been able to locate Stella Abromowitz so they've brought in the cadaver dogs and a helicopter. If you have anyone you can spare, I'm sure Pine Mountain would be glad of the help."

"Jeez," Clay said, "what's going on around here?"

"That's what we have to find out." Scoop returned his phone to his pocket. "I'll check in as soon as I'm back from Columbus."

As he hurried down the steps of the sidewalk, Hannah Sanderson drove past the hotel on her way to the museum. He dialed her number as soon as he had backed his car out of the parking space and turned it toward Columbus. It went straight to voice mail. Why had she called?

The drive would take an hour and it was nearly eight o'clock. He'd be pushing it to be back by noon but he knew it was important to see what was concerning the medical examiner. He hoped it would be worth the time it cost the investigation.

* * *

Hannah saw Scoop Russell from the corner of her eye as she drove through town. She made a point not to acknowledge that she had seen him. Dark smudges beneath her eyes gave evidence of the restless night she had endured as she struggled with what she must do to keep Teagan safe from the news frenzy that the revelation of her identify would incite. To leak vital information at this point in the investigation might jeopardize the outcome. It would be morally wrong. She took a deep, calming breath. She closed her mind to those nagging thoughts. In this instance, there were more important things than the moral high ground.

Her meeting wasn't until noon. She had debated about what to do with Teagan. It was important that no one suspect what she was planning. The best scenario would be to leave her with the girls. That way she would be away from the temptation of the murder investigation. But Phyllis had always been able to read Hannah like a book. They were all due to play a short round of golf in the late afternoon. Phyllis would see right through Hannah's sudden need of a babysitter. She didn't need that complication right now. She didn't need the hassle of defending her decision. Better to leave Teagan in Shirley's capable hands at the museum while she made her rendezvous. She would have to impress upon Shirley the importance of keeping Teagan under her watchful eye.

Besides, the museum was crawling with law enforcement and Teagan would have Fergus with her. That thought didn't comfort her as much as it should have.

After running the gauntlet of the news crews at the museum entrance, she set her mind to the problem of eliciting something new about the investigation. She knew the reporter would require something more than the party line that had been fed to the press so far. It would take something truly newsworthy if she was going to extract a promise of safety for herself and Teagan.

Chapter Eighteen

It's early still but the temperature is rising. Though the distance to the museum grounds isn't that far, I'd rather not hike it in this heat. Scoop was right in his instructions to McFadden and Birdie. The murder weapon is key to the investigation. So is the connection between D'Amboise and Rousso. He's convinced there is one and so am I. It's better I stay here on the job than ride along with Scoop in pursuit of details of the method of murder. Dead is dead. The how is known. The question is why and that won't be found in some morgue in Columbus.

Unlike Scoop, McFadden makes no complaint when I climb into the back seat of his car where he's loading his equipment. That's a wise decision on his part. Let's hope that he and Birdie let slip the reason for the sudden suspicion of Dax. I don't like Clay Bishop's eagerness to arrest him.

Something has turned their eyes in Dax's direction. I need to find out what. I fear it might be the less than friendly encounter Dax had with The Punk several days before all this nasty business of dead bodies. Someone tattled. Chivalry is overrated. Look where it has landed, Dax: under the microscope of the local law. The Man is trying to put him down, box him in, clip his wings. Wait. I'm The Man. Sort of. This is all so confusing.

Hannah and Teagan are here at the museum ahead of us, as are other members of the staff. I find that odd until I discover Shirley on a ladder in the shop with a dust cloth in her hand. She's decided to take advantage of the lack of customers by giving the place a bit of spit and polish.

I find her sharing her fears with Teagan about job security if the museum can't open for the Memorial Day crowd. Probably not the best choice of conversation to be having. I see that solemn expression on the child's face. Well, it's beyond my abilities to change the subject so I go help Teagan with a bin of miniature soldiers she's sorting. She finds my assistance more hindrance than help and laughs at my attempts. Mission accomplished.

Her mother is just about as glum as Shirley about the state of things if the dark circles under her eyes and the haunted expression on her face is any clue. She sits at her desk with her laptop open but doesn't even pretend to look at the screen. Her head is filled with dark thoughts if I'm not seriously mistaken. This is all a sad state of things.

No one else is in the museum building. I take myself on a little stroll through the main room of the exhibit. This is an amazing place. I've never in my life seen such strange contraptions. Just look at these shoes with harnesses and hinges. Almost like the gear The Farmer uses for his mule. And that's some spiffy car. I wouldn't mind a spin in that myself. But, what's this? A whole wall of dozens and dozens of carved sticks. What an odd thing. And protected, too, just like the rooms in the servants' quarters. Why anyone would bother is beyond me.

But enough of this foolishness. The day is wasting and I'm no closer to finding a killer than when this whole mess started. The answer won't be found inside the museum. I need to be outside with the search crew. At least then I'll feel like I'm accomplishing something.

* * *

Traffic was light and Scoop made good time to Columbus. The coroner was waiting for him when he arrived. He looked a little harried with his white hair mussed and his glasses perched on the tip of his nose. He did a double take at Scoop's stitches.

"That looks nasty," the coroner said.

"It'll heal."

He grunted but didn't waste any time with further pleasantries. He wheeled both bodies from storage and uncovered them. Both were face down on the gurneys.

"I wanted you to see for yourself the impressions," the coroner said. "Each one was made by a different object but both objects have very distinctive characteristics. I think that might help you find them."

They looked at the head wound on the body from Dowdell's Knob. "A thin, rectangular object about three inches long made the depression. I found leaf mold in the wound and a bit of iron rust. It came from the weapon. It was too imbedded to be from any other source." The coroner moved on to the victim's left arm. "He has a distinctive tattoo here. It has military elements. I fed it into the database to see if it's specific to any organization. Nothing popped up."

Scoop examined the tattoo. Shirley had described something very similar on the man she observed shadowing D'Amboise in the museum shop. But that man had sported a head of longish curls. The wig would explain his appearance.

They moved on to D'Amboise. "This is what's so interesting. He was struck by a rounded object, a little larger than a golf ball, I'd say, but not as big as a tennis ball. You have the curving of the indentation. But it's a very distinctive object. If you look at the bruising you see an imprint. Does that remind you of anything?"

Scoop studied the wound through a magnifying glass the coroner had pulled into place over the body. "It's a letter."

"Exactly. More specifically, it's an A."

"What would cause it?"

"I've been wracking my brain since I realized what it was. The thing that comes to mind is an old-fashioned typewriter. I used to have an IBM Selectric that had a ball engraved with raised letters of the alphabet instead of the old strike keys. It would make this kind of impression except much, much smaller."

"You think we're looking for a part from some kind of old printing press or something like that?"

"I couldn't say. Only that I can't think of anything else that would make this kind of imprint. You can see the edges of other letters on either side of the depression made by the blow."

"Huh." Scoop took out his phone and began a search for the typewriter mentioned by the coroner and found what he was talking about. He studied the depression on the back of D'Amboise's head again. "You've sent photos of this with the file?"

"Of course."

"Thanks. I'll have Birdie enlarge them and print them out for the search team." He sighed. "This could be anywhere on the mountainside."

"I can't help you there. Now," the coroner glanced at his watch and began covering the bodies, "I'm late for my golf game. I'll have my phone with me if I'm needed." He rolled D'Amboise toward the cooler. "Just don't find any more corpses today, please."

* * *

Hannah glanced at the clock. It was almost ten. She knew the CIRT team was on the premises. She had heard them when they arrived. Scoop hadn't been with them and for that she was glad. It was one thing to decide she was going to sabotage his case and quite another to have to face him without giving herself away.

She felt ashamed but knew she had to carry through with the plan. When Scoop discovered her treachery, he would never speak to her again. So be it. Teagan's emotional health was more important. Besides, the facts were bound to leak soon. They always did. Too many people knew too much about the case. It was impossible to keep everything under wraps.

The news presence was growing. She had made Teagan get into the knee well of the front seat so the photographers couldn't get a picture of her as they arrived at the museum. It had caught her by surprise to find them camped out at the entrance so early. That meant the story was gaining audience. She hoped her sunglasses made her hard to identify. Their presence and aggression meant she had to play her card while it still had value.

First things first. She needed to find McFadden or Birdie and see what new developments they had uncovered. Birdie would probably be her best bet. A sympathetic woman-to-woman chat. The fact that Teagan had been in on the discovery of D'Amboise's body played into that sisterhood vibe.

The key would be not to reveal anything to the reporter that could jeopardize the case when it came to court. She had watched enough crime shows to know there were some things the police kept back from the public. She wouldn't know what to reveal and what to conceal until she knew what developments had occurred since yesterday morning. Surely there had been something new.

She found Shirley and Teagan in the shop neatly stacking books back onto shelves. "Where's everyone?" she asked.

Shirley straightened a row of book spines. "They've decided to check all the buildings again. They're going to include the Mustian house this go 'round. The one called McFadden thinks the initial search might have been too superficial in an effort to preserve the furnishings and memorabilia from excessive handling."

"Someone should have told me."

"The Director gave them permission. Oscar phoned him. He's with the search team now. Oscar, that is, to be sure things are handled properly and put back just so."

"I could help," Teagan said. "I know where everything belongs. And all the secret places."

"You're staying right here with Shirley. There are too many people out by the entrance and heaven knows where else on the grounds."

"But, Mom—"

"No buts." Hannah didn't want to frighten Teagan but neither did she want her to wander into danger. "The police have their methods and I'm sure they won't miss anything."

The look of disappointment on Teagan's face cut Hannah to the quick but she stood firm. "I have to go out later on an errand. I'll let the detectives know where they can find me if they need me."

"Where are you going?"

"To Callaway. I need to see the cake design for Jackie's surprise party on Sunday. Chef Renee wants it to be just right. Birthdays that end in a zero or a five are always special." Hannah smiled and tweaked Teagan's nose. Then, she decided to take a calculated risk. "You want to come with me? I'm sure the girls will be happy for you to spend the afternoon with them. We have a late tee-off but we could have a swim beforehand. It'll be easy enough to swing by the house and get your swimsuit."

Teagan looked down at the book in her hand and shook her head. "Shirley needs my help."

"Suit yourself. I'll just find the detectives and let them know my plans. Won't be gone but a minute." Hannah felt a sense of relief that her ploy worked. She knew wild horses couldn't drag Teagan from the crime scene. She also felt a twinge of apprehension. Before she left to meet with the reporter, she would have to make sure Shirley understood that Teagan had to be under her watchful eye every minute.

Chapter Nineteen

Both victims were struck on the head with an object heavy enough to cause considerable damage. The problem is there are literally thousands of objects on the museum grounds that would do the job. As much as I hate to admit it, it'll take a stroke of luck to find it. Maybe even a miracle.

One thing I do know, it isn't in the servants' quarters, the garage beneath, or the guest cottage. Both McFadden and Birdie have been hard at it for some time and all they've found is a few dust bunnies.

I understand the logic of their search strategy. The killer obviously has access to the buildings of the museum. If he could get a dead body into a sealed room, he can hide a murder weapon in any of the structures that are on the site. And that's quite a few if you count the storage buildings, guard huts, and maintenance sheds. Assuming, of course, that he didn't simply give it a good toss down the mountain. I don't envy the volunteers searching the steep incline. It's a hot, sweaty job.

If we don't have the murder weapon or the location of the murder—or murders—we've hit a brick wall. So, let's look at this another way. What else isn't where it should be? Who isn't where they should be? I don't know the answer to either question but I bet Teagan does.

The problem is, how to go about asking her? That's easy enough. If I can get her out from under the watchful eye of her mother and Shirley, she'll be sticking her curious little nose into every nook and cranny in search of clues.

Her mother wants to keep her out of the investigation because she's worried for her safety. A legitimate concern, I'll grant you. Someone is ruthless enough to have killed two people. Would they hesitate at taking the life of a child? I wouldn't want to bet on it.

A tricky situation for sure.

* * *

Birdie was peeling off a pair of shoe covers when she came out the front door of the Little White House, a look of disappointment on her face. She glanced up as Hannah approached.

"Good morning." Hannah looked through the door of the house and saw that McFadden was busy on his cell phone. "Any luck?"

Birdie shook her head. "I didn't expect we'd find anything. We were careful before, but thorough. Our time would have been better spent elsewhere."

"So, nothing new? No idea of who or why?"

Birdie sighed. "No. But we do have an ID on the second body."

Hannah drew a sharp intake of breath. "A second body!"

The color rose in Birdie's cheeks. "Sorry. Probably shouldn't have let that slip."

"Who?"

For a moment Birdie hesitated, but something in Hannah's expression must have convinced her the information would be safe with her. "A man by the name of Rousso. Know him?"

Hannah shook her head.

"Found him yesterday afternoon at Dowdell's Knob. Looked like an accident at first. You know. A sightseer who took a tumble? But it was intentional."

"You mean someone pushed him?"

"Someone whacked him on the head. Just like D'Amboise. Then dropped him over the edge."

Hannah felt light-headed. What was going on in peaceful, rural Warm Springs? She took a quick breath. Here was something to give the reporter. If he didn't know already. "I didn't see anything about it on the news last night."

"For the moment the media is focused on the death in the museum. It's become quite the sensation. If anyone got wind of it, they're not being distracted by what they assume is a hiking accident. They're going all in on the significance of the inference to FDR. Is it related to him, his family. That kind of thing.

"The two different jurisdictions are working in our favor for the moment. I imagine by lunchtime someone will have let the cat out of the bag about the second body. Either here or in Pine Mountain."

"Does this death have anything to do with D'Amboise's murder?"

"That would be my guess. Unless Pine Mountain has suddenly become a hot spot of high crime. Two deaths within two days of each other isn't a coincidence. I'm sure we'll find a connection."

"Is he local? The second victim? I've been racking my brain for any memory of the name but there's nothing."

"From out of state. From what Shirley described, he was probably the man she saw tailing D'Amboise earlier in the week."

"Here? At the museum?"

Birdie made a face at the slip of the tongue then nodded.

Two men were dead. Both murdered. Both had been at the museum. Who had killed them? Had the killer been on the grounds as well? Had he crossed paths with Teagan? Now, more than ever, Hannah knew she had to keep her daughter out of the headlines. If the killer was still out there, she could be in real danger.

Birdie touched her lightly on the arm. "You okay?"

Hannah blinked. "Yes. It's just—it's just a lot to take in. I was going to leave Teagan with Shirley while I ran an errand but now—"

"Hey, it's okay. Don't get all worked up about it. This place is crawling with cops. No harm will come to Teagan."

"I don't know. She's fascinated with the mystery of the whole thing. If she should wander off—"

"I'll keep an eye on her, okay? At the moment, we're assuming that the murder scene is somewhere here. Everyone is keeping a close watch to make sure no one makes their way onto the museum grounds. This is the safest place she could be right now."

Hannah tried to feel reassured by Birdie's words. She

was probably right. If Teagan stayed at the museum, she wouldn't have to unnecessarily run the gauntlet of reporters camped out at the entrance and Hannah would be able to accomplish her mission and return quickly.

Decision made, she smiled at Birdie. "Thank you. I'll run out quickly just before noon but I'll be back in no time at all."

"No problem. I don't see us going anywhere anytime soon. Scoop should be back before then." Birdie gave her a meaningful side-eye glance as she spoke.

"Oh? Where is he?" Hannah felt the blush creeping up her cheeks.

"Columbus. Meeting with the coroner."

"Oh."

Birdie smiled and turned her full attention to her equipment bag. "Let's hope he learns something that will tell us what we need to be looking for as a murder weapon."

"Can they tell?"

"Sometimes. Apparently, there was something peculiar enough about the wound that the coroner felt Scoop should see it for himself."

"Maybe the killer took the murder weapon with him."

"That's a real possibility."

"It seems like an impossible task."

"You'd be amazed at the little details that lead to arrests that forensic science is able to identify these days. But, in this case, with no murder scene to give us direction, we'd need a real stroke of luck to find what made the wound."

Hannah didn't want to think about the wound or what kind of object could have made it. This was something that the investigators would probably want to hold back from public knowledge. It was the kind of thing that could be vital to the prosecution of the guilty party. The discovery of a second murdered body would have to be the carrot she held out for the reporter. Armed with that new information, Hannah took leave of Birdie and made her way back to the office. Now if she could only time her departure to miss Scoop's return to Warm Springs.

* * *

Scoop made good time on his return from Columbus. He decided to swing by Dowdell's Knob and check on the search for Stella Abromowitz. The coroner had determined the time of death for Rousso to be at least forty-eight to seventy-two hours prior to the discovery of the body. With the knowledge that Alice hadn't seen him at the bed and breakfast in the past three days, Scoop was leaning more toward seventy-two hours. If Abromowitz had been with Rousso, there was a definite possibility she had been thrown off the mountain, too. If that was the case, they would be looking for another corpse. Too many ifs!

So far, they had learned very little about Ms. Abromowitz. No one in the upscale New York apartment building where she lived had a clue as to where she might have gone. It wasn't that kind of building. The attendant at the garage, where she stored her car when not in use, had received a call from her to bring the car around a little less than two weeks ago. The doorman verified that the car abandoned at Dowdell's Knob was the same make and model that she drove and that he had loaded several suitcases into the trunk. From the amount of luggage, he assumed she was on her way to her summer home in Florida. He didn't know where in Florida. She had been alone when she drove away from the building.

The Pine Mountain chief was on the scene when Scoop arrived. He gave Scoop an inquiring look when he saw his injury but made no comment. He introduced him to the FBI tactical search agent in charge. The dogs had alerted on several items over the course of the morning. Rousso's wallet, empty of cash, the keys to the car, and an old, worn scythe had been retrieved.

Scoop slipped on gloves and, with cautious handling, studied the scythe. "This is the murder weapon."

"Could be," said the FBI agent. "There's blood on the blunt end where the iron of the blade protrudes through. The lab will be able to tell us who it belongs to."

"It'll match the impression on Rousso's wound, if I'm not terribly mistaken."

"My team went to the garage in Pine Mountain and examined the trunk of the abandoned car. It's being hauled back to the lab for a more thorough assessment. We're confident that the body was transported here from the murder scene in it. Any luck with that?"

"Not yet."

"Find the owner of the scythe and I'll bet you'll find your killer."

Scoop made no reply. Instead, he pictured Teagan sitting on the creek bank beside Henry Wilkes.

Chapter Twenty

I'm not sure what Hannah is up to but she seems even more stressed than earlier in the day, if that's possible. She's repeated her instructions to Shirley three times. We get it already! Teagan is to be locked down tight until she gets back. Teagan doesn't look particularly happy about it. I can't say I blame her. I, for one, have never been a fan of restrictions on my movements.

But I suppose I should put myself in the shoes of an adult in this particular situation. I remember when I was a young kitten. Poking my nose where it didn't belong cost me one of my nine lives and left me with a scarred ear. Fortunately for me, I have eight more lives. The same can't be said for Teagan so I'll have to keep a close eye on her while her mother is away on her errand. There's precious little I can do anyway, with no crime scene, no murder weapon, and no motive.

Teagan watches from the top step leading up to the museum entrance until her mother's car is out of sight. The moment Hannah turns onto Highway 27 she looks up at Shirley. "Fergus needs to go for a walk. To … you know. He hasn't been out all morning."

Cunning little wench.

Shirley eyes her and gives a small shake of her head. "I'm not that gullible, young lady."

"Honest. He needs a walk. You can come with us."

"I think I just might."

Teagan shrugs. "Fine."

"Fine."

I gather from the tone of voice that this is a subtle battle of wills so I take no position in the outcome. It's a known fact that dogs need to walk so Shirley was on the losing end of this proposition from the get-go. She jerks her head in the direction of the museum entrance. The three of them troop through the door, into the shop, and out through the gallery displaying FDR's portrait. I trail along behind because I know what our young sleuth has in mind.

We all head in the direction of the public restroom and the stand of trees beyond. This, apparently, is Fergus' preferred spot to "walk."

Since I will do the decent thing and give him privacy to commune with nature, I decide to check on the progress of the CIRT team. Birdie is sitting on the steps of the guest cottage making notes on a diagram of the museum grounds.

I settle beside her and look at the scribblings on the map. I assume they indicate the areas that have been searched and what was found or, in this case, not found. Birdie looks tired and a little dispirited. I would cheer her up if I could but I suspect the only thing that would lift her spirits would be a clue about the crime.

Birdie sighs and looks at me. "Got any ideas?" *she asks.*

Unfortunately, I don't, so I climb onto her lap and settle down.

She scratches under my chin. "We're just chasing our tails. If I had some idea as to motive maybe it would point us in a direction." *She leans against the door frame of the guest cottage.* "Why here? Why all the theatrics of the locked room?"

I look up at her. I think she's onto something.

"What is the killer trying to draw attention to? To someone at the museum?" *She becomes very still.* "It's about the family. The Roosevelt family."

Could that be the case? A lot of effort went into getting the body into the room. The murderer would know this would sensationalize the discovery, that everyone would be scrambling to find a connection. So, if Birdie's right, it's all a sleight-of-hand trick to make us look in a certain direction. What, then, is that direction? What message is the killer trying to send?

* * *

A sense of urgency made Scoop take the curves down Pine Mountain at a reckless speed. The thought of Henry Wilkes as the murderer didn't sit well with him but he had to concede that it was within the realm of possibility. The scythe wasn't a convenient murder weapon. The long wooden handle made it unwieldy. It would be difficult for anyone who wasn't accustomed to handling it to use it easily.

Wilkes was protective of the museum and the memory of FDR. Teagan had revealed that he'd spent his whole life caring for the place. What could D'Amboise have said or done that would enrage Wilkes enough to lash out? And why leave the body on the premises? The smart thing would be to obscure the connection with the museum. Plus,

Wilkes had given the murder weapon up by mentioning it in their interview. Or he had been covering his tracks.

Scoop was working at this knotty question as he came out of a sharp curve and met Hannah headed in the opposite direction. He flew past her almost before he recognized the car. Had Teagan been with her? He didn't think so.

Quickly he dialed her phone. After several rings it went to voice mail. She was avoiding him. Why?

He couldn't worry about that now. He needed to locate Henry Wilkes.

Could Wilkes be a threat to the child? He didn't know.

* * *

Hannah's heart skipped a beat when she recognized Scoop's car barreling down the road toward her. She glanced in the rearview mirror as he flew past and breathed a sigh of relief when he didn't so much as pump the brakes. Then her phone rang. She glanced down at the number. He was calling her.

She tightened her grip on the steering wheel. There was no way she would be able to keep her nerve and follow through with her plan if she talked to him. Deep in her gut she felt he would somehow know she was up to something.

How ridiculous, she thought. I've hardly ever spoken more than a few dozen words to the man. But, still, she knew she couldn't fool him. She couldn't trust herself not to give the game away.

Why was fate so cruel? Wasn't it enough that she and Teagan had to endure the loss of husband and father? To have been at the mercy of overzealous reporters who would do anything to sensationalize their tragedy still haunted both of them. It was all starting up again. Hannah couldn't allow it. She just couldn't.

The beach entrance onto the grounds of Callaway Gardens would be the best way to reach the butterfly house without attracting attention. That way Hannah wouldn't have to pass by the information center and prying eyes.

She drove past the Big Top, Robin Lake, and along the twisting lane through the golf course to her destination. There were a number of cars in the parking lot but nothing that distinguished itself as a news affiliate's vehicle.

She checked the time. Just over ten minutes until the rendezvous. The rear of the parking lot offered some shelter from the sun and she parked there. As she walked across the lot, she checked all the cars. No one was sitting idly waiting. If she was lucky, she was ahead of the reporter.

Instead of entering the exhibit through the main entrance into the high atrium that housed the plants, fountains, and pools that created the habitat for the wide variety of butterflies, she slipped into the shop and then through the exit door of the butterfly house. The vegetation and waterfalls partially screened her from the tourists marveling at the butterflies flitting all around. The reporter had the advantage of knowing what she looked like. She wanted to spot him before she went any further with this assignation.

As she made her way around tall foliage in a reverse path, she spied him. Just as she had thought, he was the one person watching the entrance to the atrium rather than marveling at the delicate creatures fluttering through the air.

Chase Gibbons was the man who had been table

hopping at The Bulloch House Restaurant. He glanced down at his cell phone and appeared to be reading a message. Had she left it too late? Was he, at this moment, being made aware of the second body? If so, her bargaining chip would have no value.

"Mr. Gibbons," she said as she approached him.

He turned, slid the phone into his pocket, and said, "Mrs. Sanderson. I was beginning to think you weren't coming."

"It's only just now twelve."

"True. Should we go somewhere so we can talk privately?"

"No. The waterfall will keep our conversation private enough."

"But it makes for a poor recording."

"There won't be a recording."

"I need to be able to substantiate my sources."

"I don't recall that being a necessity, only a convenience."

His brows shot up and he nodded. "I can understand your reluctance. I imagine the death of your husband was a very trying time for you."

"Can we skip the insincere platitudes and get this over with?"

He studied her a moment, glanced around the atrium, then motioned toward a secluded area several feet away. Once they were ensconced with their backs to the glass exterior wall, he took out a notebook and gave her a fleeting smile. "Old school it shall be."

When Hannah made no response, he cleared his throat. "Who found the body of D'Amboise? The rumor is that it was a group of kids from outside the area."

"I don't know where they were from. I didn't recognize

any of them."

"Do you have their names?"

"No. The police will have that information. But I doubt they'll share it. They're minors, after all."

"How old were they?"

"Probably between the ages of eight to ten."

"And what exactly did they find?"

Now was the moment. How much could she reveal without risking the ability of the police to apprehend of the killer? Would the location of the body give away too much information?

"Come on, Mrs. Sanderson. It's no secret that a dead body was found in one of the buildings of the museum. The rumor is that he was murdered. The exact building isn't going to give away anything that isn't already common knowledge."

"He was in the servants' cottage."

"Where in the servants' cottage?"

"On the bed."

Gibbons glanced up at her, his pen poised over the notepad. "That's interesting. What was the manner of death?"

"I couldn't say."

"You didn't see the body?"

Again, she hesitated.

"You might as well tell me. I understand that one of the security guards for the museum was on hand."

Oscar. What had he revealed?

"Before we go any further, Mr. Gibbons, we need to have an understanding."

"About revealing your identity."

"Yes."

"I can assure you that your secret's safe with me."

"Then why don't I feel reassured?"

Gibbons glanced away from her penetrating regard. "Look, I know you had a rough time with the news coverage of your husband's death. I get that you don't want to relive that experience. I'm not the enemy here. I'm just doing my job. And that job is to get the story. This story. About a dead body at the FDR museum."

"If I give you something that no one else knows, will you promise to keep my name out of it? Will you swear you won't decide a rehash of David's death would add to the newsworthiness of this death at the museum?"

"I swear. I'll keep it under wraps. If this story involves one of FDR's descendants, that's all I'll need for the top of the hour story."

"What makes you think it's related to one of the Roosevelts?"

"Joyce Favor. She was at the bed and breakfast for over a week."

"Who is Joyce Favor?"

"A direct descendant of Roosevelt."

"And you think that has something to do with this death?"

"D'Amboise was dogging her footsteps. Why would he do that? And how did he know who she was? I smell a story."

If what Gibbons was saying was true, it would mean an onslaught of media coverage for the foreseeable future. Could she keep her identity hidden under such circumstances?

Gibbons' phone vibrated. He glanced down.

"There's another body," Hannah blurted out.

Gibbon's head jerked up. "What? At the museum?

Who is it?"

"Not at the museum." Hannah wanted to limit the damage of her betrayal as much as possible. "It might not be related. But two bodies in two days—"

"Where?"

"Dowdell's Knob. The Pine Mountain police are in charge of the investigation. That's why no one has made the connection."

"You think they're connected?"

"I have no idea. It just seems strange to have two deaths on park lands in such close proximity."

Gibbons had his phone out and was furiously texting. "When was it discovered?"

"Yesterday afternoon."

"Manner of death?"

"I don't know. It was initially thought to be an accident. A fall from the lookout point."

Gibbons looked at her, a gleam of anticipation in his eye. "But?"

"It wasn't an accident."

"How do you know this?"

She stared at him in return. "I have to protect my sources."

He grinned. "Thank you, Mrs. Sanderson," he said as he put the phone to his ear and began walking toward the exit.

"Remember, we have a deal," Hannah called after him.

He gave a wave of his hand as he spoke into his phone.

All Hannah could do now was hope he would be good at his word. The idea that a member of the Roosevelt family might be somehow involved in whatever was happening in Warm Springs was both a relief and a worry. If it was true, the focus of the news coverage would take a different turn, away from the people of Warm Springs. They'd be digging into the possibility of a scandal in the Roosevelt family. It would heat up interest in the murder.

But that direction was a double-edged sword. It could potentially put everyone connected to the museum under the microscope. They would become targets of anyone looking to score a headline. Either way, she would have to tread lightly until the furor over the murders subsided.

Murders. A chill ran down her spine.

Chapter Twenty-One

Apparently, Fergus is in a mood to explore. He comes bounding toward me and Birdie from over the small rise. Teagan and Shirley aren't far behind. I've no doubt this turn of events is delighting Teagan. But Shirley doesn't seem to be put out by the diversion from a day of dusting and sorting.

I suspect Shirley is as curious as Teagan about the state of the investigation although she doesn't let it show. And who wouldn't be? A murder on your doorstep? How often does that happen?

Shirley pulls a bottle of cold water from her knapsack and gives it to Birdie. "Thought you might be a little thirsty."

Ah, so Shirley is the instigator of this little side excursion. As they say, curiosity killed the cat. Why they say that is beyond me. It's one of those strange human oddities that really makes no sense. I mean, seriously, I've been curious all my life and yet here I am, still above ground.

I'd be the last one to reprimand Shirley for her curiosity, though, since her questions will surely lead to any revelations about the case. I'm not one to look a gift horse in the mouth. Whatever that means. Really, I think I've been spending too much time around The Farmer and his Wife. I'm beginning to sound just like them.

"Any luck?" *Shirley asks.*

Birdie shakes her head. "Do you remember anything D'Amboise was asking about the Roosevelts? Anything that would suggest he was looking for something specific?"

"He did ask about the family and their involvement in the museum. Wanted to know if any of them served on the board or had an interest in the running of things."

"And?"

Shirley shrugs. "I told him no. The compound was given to the state of Georgia after the death of the President. On very rare occasions, one or another of his descendants would come by to tour the place. The Director usually shows them around."

Birdie's brow furrowed as she considered this little tidbit. "Did he ask about anyone by name?"

"He asked me about Joyce Favor."

"Who's Joyce Favor?"

"A great-great niece, or something like that. She didn't say specifically."

"You spoke with her?"

Shirley nodded. "She used her credit card to purchase a compass with the museum logo on it. I recognized the name from the genealogy chart and asked if she was related."

Here, at last, is something to sink my teeth into. A member of the Roosevelt family was lately staying at the bed and breakfast and suddenly checked out early. But what is the significance of it?

* * *

Fergus came bounding toward him as Scoop walked over the rise. The dog danced excitedly around his feet as he made his way to the trio of Birdie, Shirley, and Teagan. He felt the tension in his shoulders ease as they came into view.

Teagan ran to him and took his hand as they continued toward the guest cottage. "We have a clue!"

"Do you?"

"Yes. The dead guy wanted to know about President Roosevelt's great-great niece!"

"Who is President Roosevelt's great-great niece?"

"Joyce Favor," all three of them answered in unison.

Alice's posh guest at the bed and breakfast who had conveniently checked out in the morning before the discovery of D'Amboise's body. The guest who was still to be interviewed.

"Where did you learn this?"

"From Shirley. He was asking Shirley about her."

Scoop looked at Shirley. "Why didn't you tell me this before?"

"I didn't know that it had anything to do with his murder. I told you he wanted to know about the Roosevelts and didn't seem much interested in the museum." She shrugged. "And to be truthful, I didn't remember him asking about her until Birdie wanted to know if he had mentioned anyone specific."

"How did you know Joyce Favor was related to the Roosevelts?"

"It's in the genealogy chart in the museum. Not her specifically, but there's a breakdown of the family chart and Favor is one of the family names."

Scoop gave himself a mental kick in the pants. The possibility that the death could be in some way associated with a member of the Roosevelt family had never been a serious consideration. The family had no connection to the museum. It had been a state-run facility for decades. He had even begun to suspect the location of the body had all been a ruse to misdirect attention from the true motive and murderer.

As his mind examined this possibility, he watched the gray cat saunter down the slope and through the open doorway of the Little White House as McFadden emerged, a look of annoyance on his face.

"There's a reporter at the Pine Mountain police station," he said as he crossed the outer circle to join Scoop and the others on the bricked patio. "He's asking questions about the body found on Dowdell's Knob."

"It was bound to get out. I'm surprised that it took this long."

"Yeah, but the difference is this guy says he has a source that confirms the two deaths are connected and that they're both murder victims."

Scoop repressed the expletive on the tip of his tongue when he remembered Teagan's presence. "Who's his source?"

McFadden shook his head. "You know the old song and dance. Privileged information."

Teagan tugged Scoop's hand. "There's another murder?"

He looked into her earnest gaze and knew he had to be truthful with her. "Yes. We thought it was an accident but

I'm afraid it isn't. He was struck in the back of the head like D'Amboise."

"Who leaked?" Her expression was dead serious and a little murderous.

Scoop's brows shot up but he kept a straight face and said, "I don't know. A lot of people were involved in the recovery."

"It won't be anyone from Warm Springs." Her expression was one of great conviction.

"Why do you say that?"

"You said not to tell."

"People don't always listen when I tell them things."

"No one at the museum would tell. We protect the memory of the Roosevelts."

Henry Wilkes popped into Scoop's mind as she uttered those words. Did all the employees of the museum feel as strongly about the Roosevelt family? He mentally ran down the list of museum employees and local people who had been involved in the search for the scene of the crime and the murder weapon. Could one of them be involved?

He dismissed the thought. More likely, one of them had been the source of the leak. Teagan's loyalty and trust were refreshing but probably misplaced. "Why don't you go inside and find the cat. He's in there poking his nose where it doesn't belong."

* * *

Hannah drove through the twists and turns of Callaway Gardens to the lodge. She had told Teagan that she was going to check on Jackie's birthday cake and she wanted at least that much of her excuse to be true. Chef Renee was surprised when she walked into the kitchen.

"I came to view the cake." Hannah hoped her smile seemed genuine.

"Okay. But it's a long way from being finished. I usually don't do the final design until the morning of the event."

"That's fine. I just promised Teagan I'd take a peek at it."

"Well, we don't want to disappoint Teagan."

Chef Renee pulled the two-tier cake from the industrial refrigerator. It looked very plain with white icing hiding the chocolate-raspberry filling. Only a single row of @ symbols served to form a border around the bottom layer. Hannah knew it would be great. Not only was it meant to celebrate Jackie's birthday, but to congratulate her dear friend on the success of her website business. Teagan would be tickled with the high-tech design.

"Looks great."

"Well, it *will* look great when it's finished. You want to take a photo for Teagan?"

Hannah shook her head. "No. I'll let her enjoy the surprise when we unveil it at the celebration."

She stopped in Carson's Tap Room and ordered sandwiches to go. She was aware she was killing time, hoping against hope that Scoop wouldn't be at the museum when she returned. The moment Chase Gibbons told her his suspicions about a connection between D'Amboise and the Roosevelt family, she knew she would have to tell Scoop about it. If any of it was true, Scoop needed to know. And he needed to know before the reporter splashed it across every available media outlet.

It was getting on toward one o'clock when she took the sandwiches and made the drive back to the museum. Just as she feared, Scoop's vehicle was in the parking lot.

Chapter Twenty-Two

Yes, curiosity is my middle name. After all, an open door is an open invitation, right? It's interesting to see what people find so fascinating about the Little White House. I suppose if The Farmer's Wife had to cook in this tiny kitchen with no modern conveniences she wouldn't be so giving when it comes to meal time. I can imagine it was quite a job to provide a meal befitting someone of the President's status, especially if there were guests.

As for me, I like the simple life. A cozy place to snooze, a tasty handout, the follies of humans to entertain me. Who could ask for more?

Well, I admit, double murders in our sleepy little town have certainly upped the excitement around here. I'm afraid it'll be rather dull once the case is solved. How does the old song go? "How ya gonna keep 'em down on the farm after they've seen Parée'." Yep, mighty dull, indeed.

I do believe this is quite the smallest bed I've ever seen. Not that I've spent a lot of time in people's houses. If Roosevelt was as tall a man as they say he was, I can't imagine how he slept on this thing. To each his own. As for me, a nice chair cushion and I'm out like a light.

Everything in here is small but there seem to be all the usual things humans find necessary. And, what's this? Well, well. It's one of those carved sticks. There's something decidedly different about this one, though. My nose twitches and I sniff it all along the length to the rounded knob at the top. There. There is the foul thing.

"Callahan."

Teagan's voice startles me, so focused am I on the carved stick and the story it tells. She moves closer and becomes very still. "You've found it," *she says in a hushed voice.*

And so I have.

* * *

Scoop, Birdie, and McFadden all stared at the carved walking cane leaning against the wall in the dim corner of the room near the head of Roosevelt's bed. It was barely distinguishable from the dark wood of the walls.

"I'm sorry, Boss." McFadden sounded lower than a snake's belly. He fiddled with the camera he had used to take photos of the cane in place, the space beneath the bed, and just about every other inch of the room. "I just thought it was part of the museum display to make it all look authentic. There are dozens of them in the display case."

Birdie kept glancing anxiously at Scoop's face but made no comment.

Scoop pulled on a pair of gloves, sidled into the tight

space between bed and wall, and gripped the cane near the bottom to carefully lift it from its resting place. Once he moved toward the light coming in from the window on the other side of the very small room, you could see the distinctive carving. The coroner had been right. The carved letters reminded him of a giant IBM Selectric typewriter ball. The only difference was there was only one line of lettering carved around the circumference of the head of the cane. As he and his two technicians examined it, the capital letter A was partly obscured by dried blood as was the letter W to the left of the A and the letter S to the right of the A.

On his phone, Scoop pulled up the photo of the wound from the coroner's file. This was the murder weapon. There was no doubt about it.

"Sorry, Boss," Birdie said in a low voice.

"Don't beat yourself up. It was barely visible against the wood of the wall. You couldn't tell there was anything on it." He handed the cane to Birdie. "It's like Mac said, it looks like part of the normal exhibit. Teagan realized it didn't belong here because she's so familiar with everything on the premises."

"It was Callahan," Teagan said.

The three adults turned at the sound of her voice.

"Callahan was sniffing it when I came looking for him. He knew it didn't belong here. I knew it, too. It's one of the canes from the museum display case."

Scoop thought about how the canes were displayed. There was no obvious way to access them. They were all attached to the back wall of the display case in the main room of the FDR exhibit. The glass fronts of the cases were seamless. Just like the bedroom door in the servants' quarters where the killer had stashed the body, only the cases didn't appear to have hinged doors. They needed to have a closer look.

Birdie dug two large paper bags from her kit and secured them over the cane. Once she got it back to the incident room at the police station, she would swab it and get the sample to the lab ASAP. But none of them had any doubt that this was the murder weapon and that this blood would prove to belong to Curtis Arthur D'Amboise.

Scoop glanced at his watch. The day was slipping away. Friday traffic between Warm Springs and Atlanta would be a slow slog and he didn't want to waste another day getting the cane to the lab. He also didn't want to disrupt the chain of evidence. Birdie would go with it.

He dug in his pocket for the card for the FBI field agent. The agent answered on the first ring. To everyone's relief, Stella Abromowitz had been found and not on the mountainside. She was a guest at the Lodge at Callaway Gardens and had been for the past three days under a different name. The hotel clerk realized this was the person the police had been asking about when she tried to check out using her credit card.

Fortunately, the search and rescue helicopter had not yet taken off. The agent in charge was happy to give Birdie and the cane a lift.

That settled, Birdie set out on a mad dash to Pine Mountain while Scoop and McFadden made their way to the main display room of the museum.

As they scrutinized the long row of walking canes, they discovered the spot that had once housed the murder weapon. Because of the irregular shapes of the canes, due to their elaborate carvings and styles, they were displayed in an irregular pattern to save space and accommodate those features. That was why no one had noticed one was missing.

"Did he pick a cane at random? Or does this particular one have significance to the killer? That's what we need to know." Scoop let his gaze travel over the seams of the glass inserts in the cabinet face. No way did the killer access the cane this way.

The display was lit from above through an opaque sheet of what looked like Plexiglass. "Anyone have a ladder?"

"There's one in the shop. Shirley's been using it to reach the top shelves to dust." Teagan tore off in the direction of the museum shop. McFadden followed on her heels.

Scoop stared at the clear plastic clips that had held the cane in place. They wouldn't be noticed unless someone was looking specifically at the individual canes on display. He gave free rein to the rage that had been building since the discovery of the murder weapon. The killer was toying with them. Playing some kind of sick game. He was flaunting his deed, certain that he was too clever to be caught.

I will catch you, Scoop silently vowed.

Chapter Twenty-Three

If the look of thunder on Scoop's face is anything to go by, some hapless soul is in for a drubbing. I wouldn't want to be the next person to cross his path. I can understand his frustration. To have the murder weapon in plain sight and for his team to have missed it—twice—is a black eye that will sting for some time to come. Not that I blame Birdie or McFadden. We are in a museum, after all, and humans are peculiar in their need to recreate the past. It was perfectly logical to assume the cane was meant to be exactly where it was. If not for my keen sense of smell, the murder weapon would probably still be sitting exactly where the killer placed it.

Or perhaps not. Teagan has a sharp eye, an inquisitive mind, and an intimate knowledge of everything on the compound. I've no doubt she would have spied the misplaced object the next time she came through the house. But that could have been far into the future if I had not decided to satisfy my curiosity. My fatal flaw comes to the rescue. Curiosity did not kill the cat. It revealed the murder weapon.

Scoop wanders away from the display of canes as he scrutinizes various placards and objects attached to the walls. He stops before one that has a photo of Roosevelt and a diagram of connected notes. He studies them intensely.

The sound of the front door of the museum closing causes him to look to his left. Hannah has returned from her errand.

She glances down the corridor toward us and stops. Then she walks in our direction. The look on her face isn't much happier than Scoop's. I fear this doesn't bode well.

* * *

"Hello," Hannah said.

"Hannah," Scoop replied.

Her forehead creased with concern when she saw the stitches on his head. "What happened to you?"

"It's nothing for you to be concerned about."

He knows, Hannah thought. Nothing else could explain the expression on his face, the curt tone of his voice.

She stood a little taller. Better to get it over with, she decided.

"There's something you need to know." She swallowed. "A reporter knows about the other body."

"So I've been informed."

"I'm sorry."

"So am I. But with reporters crawling all over the place, it was bound to leak."

"Oh. I thought—" She hesitated.

"Thought what?"

"You'd be angry with me."

"Why? It's not your fault."

He *didn't* know. She stared into his eyes as she fought the impulse to confess. Here was an opportunity to dodge the bullet. If she kept her mouth shut, she could escape his wrath and disappointment. In that moment she knew she really, really wanted to escape his disappointment much more than his anger. But there were things he needed to know about the case, things she could tell him, and in the telling she would reveal her culpability. Her better self knew she had to tell him.

"There's more. He's found a connection between the two deaths and the Roosevelt family."

Scoop narrowed his eyes. "He?"

Hannah swallowed and nodded. "Yes. Chase Gibbons. He thinks D'Amboise was somehow connected to Joyce Favor, a descendant of the Roosevelts."

"And how do you know this?"

She could feel the tears forming at the back of her eyes and willed them into abeyance. "Because I met with him about a half hour ago." She felt a little faint at the expression on his face. "I'm the one who told him about the connection between D'Amboise and the second body."

For a full minute, he didn't speak. Finally, he asked, "Why would you do that?"

"I had to."

"Had to?"

"It's complicated."

At that moment, Teagan and McFadden arrived with the ladder from the shop.

Hannah watched as a calm, cool look settled over Scoop's features. He turned from her and walked around FDR's roadster to the other side of the pony wall that held the display of Roosevelt's walking canes.

"Mom, Mom!" Teagan squealed as she danced around in front of her, "I found a clue!"

Fergus was wagging his whole body, Teagan's excitement energizing both of them.

Hannah tried for a smile. Apparently, it was successful enough that in her excitement, Teagan didn't realize anything was wrong.

"It was a walking stick! One of the President's walking sticks from the display case." She was grinning from ear to ear. "And I found it." She gave a little bob of her head. "Well, actually, Callahan found it. But I knew what it meant!"

"Well, we'd better watch out. If we're not careful they'll be giving you a badge and a magnifying glass."

"Oh, Mom!"

But Teagan was grinning from ear to ear and for that Hannah was thankful. She couldn't remember when she'd last seen her so excited and happy about anything.

"Come on," Teagan said as she grabbed her mother's hand. "We're going to figure out how he got it out of the case."

But when they rounded the corner to the display case, Scoop looked down from the top of the ladder. "I think, Mrs. Sanderson, it might be best if you took Teagan to your office. A murder investigation isn't the most suitable place for a child."

And just like that, the light went out of Teagan's eyes and the smile slipped from her face.

Hannah was so angry she could have pushed the ladder out from under him. How dare he crush Teagan's happiness because he was annoyed with her.

She swooped Teagan into her arms and turned from

the room. She would not let him see the hurt in her child's face or the outrage in hers.

* * *

Scoop knew the moment the words were out of his mouth that he had been too harsh. By giving in to his anger at the events of the day and Hannah, he had wounded Teagan. Deeply. McFadden wouldn't meet his gaze and that told Scoop more than words could that he had screwed up royally.

It didn't matter, he told himself. She *was* a child and she didn't need to be involved in a double homicide. He should have never allowed her to be anywhere near the investigation. Asserting the truth of the situation didn't make him feel any better.

He needed to focus on the case and forget everything else. They had three solid clues and a bunch of possible scenarios. Stick with the tangibles. The scythe, the walking cane, and the bit of torn fabric. Those things would lead him to the killer.

He had long since discounted an outsider. This was someone from Warm Springs who knew the museum as well as Teagan, if not better. Someone who had known how to get the cane out of the display. The killer thought he was smarter than Scoop. Smarter than everyone. And that was a very revealing clue in and of itself. The killer had a need to flaunt his prowess. It would, Scoop decided, lead to his downfall.

And when he caught him, Scoop would leave Warm Springs behind without a backward glance. He didn't need the complications that the reappearance of Hannah Wilson in his life brought. He needed to solve the case and make his flight to Cancun.

He found the top of the display case to be the access point to get to the walking canes. Fluorescent lights were mounted on top of the opaque Plexiglass but both were easily removed. The cabinets were too shallow for anyone to descend into them but it looked possible to reach down and extract a cane without too much trouble. Scoop could see the marks in the dust where the killer had been before him. It was important not to disturb anything until McFadden had photographed all of it and did a thorough search for fingerprints. He climbed down the ladder and relinquished it to McFadden.

Scoop made his way to the break room. It was empty. He checked the coffee pot but the contents were stone cold. He took a bottle of water from the refrigerator and sat at the table he was using for a desk. His head was pounding.

With a sigh, he unlocked his phone and began to scroll through the dozens of messages. He stopped at the one from his brother. It was short and sweet. *Check your email.*

His inbox was full of emails. He scrolled down to the one from his brother. There was no subject and no message, just two attachments. One was labeled Sanderson and the other Daxter.

He opened the one on Sergeant Benjamin Matthew Daxter. It was a concise government document detailing his career with the Army from enlistment to discharge. There wasn't anything unusual other than the fact he had been wounded in Afghanistan. The wound hadn't been major, a bit of shrapnel through the calf of his right leg. It had been enough to pull him out of the field. A year and a half later his enlistment ended and he didn't re-up for a third stint. There was no indication of any disciplinary issues. All reports from his commanding officer had been to the effect that he was a good soldier who served his country well.

He stared at the file labeled Sanderson. He would be leaving Warm Springs as soon as the investigation was finished. Did he really want to go there?

It didn't matter if he did or not, he needed to. For the sake of the case if nothing else. He tapped the link and an email filled with links opened up. After viewing the third one, Scoop didn't need to look at any more. He now knew why Hannah was so apprehensive about all the attention the investigation was creating around the museum. He felt like a real dog.

Chapter Twenty-Four

I think the old expression "you could cut the air with a knife" is appropriate to the atmosphere here at the museum. McFadden looks about as glum as a guy can be. Scoop is like a pacing thundercloud, and Hannah is trying hard to conceal the fact that she's about to explode.

If you ask me, it all goes back to the fact that humans spend way too much time second-guessing their actions and motives. Unlike cats, they get all bound up in emotions and issues of integrity, honesty, and morality. It's depressing just thinking about it. If only they would act on pure instinct, we wouldn't have all these minefields to tiptoe around.

It looks like Scoop has decided to wave the white flag. He has taken a juice box and another bottle of water from the refrigerator in the break room. He finds Hannah and Teagan in the office.

Hannah looks up then quickly away. Teagan is slumped in the corner with Fergus half-in and half-out of her lap. She glances at Scoop then back at her iPad.

Scoop stands in the doorway, drinks in hand. He's hesitant, then takes a step into the room. "I'm sorry."

He's looking at Teagan but I get the impression that the apology is for Hannah as well.

"I let my anger at my own bungling spill over onto you, Teagan." *He approaches her and hands her the juice box. The water bottle he places on Hannah's desk.*

Teagan sits up straighter but her lip is still poked out far enough to serve as a bookshelf.

"The truth is," *Scoop says as he pulls a chair over to where she sits on the floor,* "I've been impressed with your sharp eye and your skills of observation since we first met. We wouldn't have our most important clue if it wasn't for you."

Teagan's lip is no longer as protruding and she jabs the straw into the juice box.

"I realize you know the museum grounds better than anyone and you're good at listening and watching. Both are essential to a good detective."

She sits up straighter still and sips from the juice box.

"I thought you might want to see what McFadden found on top of the display case. And then maybe we could take Fergus for a walk."

Teagan looks from Scoop to Hannah, who has been watching the exchange between the two of them. The pleading look in Teagan's expression causes her to give a slight nod.

Fergus is unceremoniously dumped from her lap as Teagan gets to her feet and runs from the room, Fergus at her heels.

A silence follows her departure. Scoop watches Hannah as she pretends to be engrossed in something on her laptop.

"Why didn't you tell me about David?"

Ah, what is this? Who is David?

Hannah looks up, then quickly away from the kindness she sees in his eyes. She simply shakes her head.

"The reporter threatened to make your identity public, didn't he?" *I hear the repressed anger in Scoop's voice. It seems everyone involved in this investigation doesn't give two straws for reporters. What malignant power do they have that makes them so despised?*

"He promised he wouldn't reveal the connection if I gave him something important."

"You should have come to me."

"Why? So you could tell him to leave us alone? Fat lot of good that would do." *Oh, dear. Tears are forming in her eyes.* "They don't care. They don't care about anything but a headline. No matter if it's true or not. I couldn't expose Teagan to that again."

Now we're getting to the heart of the matter. Reporters somehow pose a threat to Teagan and it's all because of this mysterious David. What did he do?

Scoop stands and crosses the room. "Come on," *he says.* "Let's collect Teagan and Fergus for that walk. I need to leave in a few minutes for Pine Mountain."

For a moment I think she's going to ask why, which would be helpful. But she doesn't. Foiled again. Instead, she rises from her chair and joins him as they go in search of Teagan. And I am left with another puzzle. This case keeps getting curiouser and curiouser. David? Pine Mountain? What does it all mean?

We find our budding detective on top of the ladder leaning over the edge of the display cabinet.

"Teagan!" *Hannah exclaims.* "You're going to fall!"

Teagan's head pops up from whatever she's looking at.

"It's a fingerprint! McFadden found a fingerprint."

* * *

Hannah watched Teagan playing a game on her iPad. For the moment, the case was forgotten. If only they could go back in time, she thought. If they could simply undo the past three days. At that moment Billy Brad stuck his head through the door of her office.

"Hey."

Hannah smiled. She really needed to do something to thank him for fixing her outdoor lights. "Hey, Billy Brad."

Fergus had scrambled to his feet at the sound of his voice. He took a stance in front of Teagan and gave a low woof.

"Fergus!" Hannah rose from her desk. "Sorry about that, Billy Brad. I think all the strangers and unsettled routine of the last couple of days has him confused."

"It's okay," Billy Brad said. "I was just looking for the top cop. Wanted to run down the gist of the interviews with everyone in town with him."

"You haven't interviewed everyone, have you?"

Billy Brad gave a shake of his head. "Pretty much. You never know who's going to remember something and apparently this D'Amboise fella was poking his nose in everywhere."

"That's a major undertaking."

"Tell me about it." He remained in the doorway as they talked.

"Did you find any clues?" Teagan asked.

"Well," Billy Brad drawled, "he broke a ceramic Scottie in the Bluebird Cottage and refused to pay for it. Bobbie

Jean wasn't very pleased about that."

Hannah was watching Teagan. She matched Billy Brad's lighthearted tone. "Now if that isn't a sign of poor character, I don't know what is."

"Indeed."

Teagan made no comment. She returned her attention to her video game, apparently losing interest in the exchange.

"So, where's the CIRT detective?" Billy Brad asked.

"You just missed him. Pine Mountain."

"Oh, yeah? What's up?"

Hannah shrugged. "He didn't say." She felt the heat rising in her cheeks. Scoop hadn't said, because she was untrustworthy. But Billy Brad didn't know that. "You should call him."

Teagan looked up from her iPad. "We found a clue."

Billy Brad took a step into the room. "Yeah?" Teagan nodded. "A fingerprint."

"That's impressive. Where did you find it?"

"On the display case for the walking sticks."

He was silent for a moment, studying Teagan. "I imagine there are dozens of fingerprints on the display case."

"Not on the top of the case."

"What made them look up there?"

"Because I found the murder weapon."

"Huh."

"Scoop will find the murderer. He's very good."

"I'm glad to hear it. All this excitement is getting a little old. I'm ready for us to go back to our boring old peace and quiet."

"So am I," Hannah said.

Billy Brad smiled and dipped his chin as he turned to the door. "You young ladies stay safe. I'll go track down that detective but, if it's as you say, Teagan, I don't think he'll need much help from the likes of me."

Once Billy Brad was out of earshot, Hannah turned to Teagan.

"I don't think you should be telling people you found the walking stick, Teagan."

"Why?"

"Well, sometimes it's best to keep the clues secret."

"But not from Billy Brad."

Hannah conceded that Billy Brad and the rest of the Warm Springs police force would know about the discovery of the murder weapon shortly if they didn't already. They would also know that Teagan was the one who found it.

She was being too protective.

But someone inside the investigation had leaked information to Gibbons. Could it be Billy Brad?

Surely not.

* * *

Stella Abromowitz was something to behold. She was a tall woman, at least six feet, and what some would call big boned. Very fit. If he were to guess, Scoop would put her age at mid to late forties. Everything about her looked expensive from the manicured nails to the bold jewelry and the expensively casual jeans and man-tailored silk blouse. She had a head of long, streaked blonde hair worn in a jumbled mess of curls. The style reminded him of an old film starring Raquel Welch in a lion skin outfit. That pretty much summed up Stella.

She paced the interview room like a caged tiger.

"I still don't know why I'm here. I'm due back in New York tomorrow morning for a very important appointment."

The Pine Mountain police chief sat back in his chair, hands clasped behind his head and watched her pacing through narrowed eyes.

"Because your automobile was found at the scene of a murder. And until you can explain that to my satisfaction, you're not going anywhere."

She looked from the chief to Scoop where he stood against the back wall of the interview room. Finally, she pulled out a chair and sat. "I loaned it to someone, okay? I'm in a rental because he didn't bring it back."

"Bring it back where?"

For a moment she looked surprised by the question. "Sarasota."

"What were you doing in Sarasota?"

"I have a place there. I like to spend time down there in the winter months and during the racing season."

"Horse racing?"

"Yes."

"You like betting on horses?"

"I like owning horses."

"Same difference."

She shrugged. "I guess you could look at it that way."

Scoop crossed the room and pulled out a chair across from Stella. "That's an expensive hobby."

"So?"

"You buy any horses lately?"

"I'm always buying horses. And selling them."

"How is Anthony Rousso involved?"

"I already told the first cop, I don't know who you're talking about."

"Sure you do. You loaned him your car."

Scoop could almost see the wheels turning.

She sighed. "He hangs around the track. Sometimes he runs errands for people. He's good at finding things."

"Things like con men?"

She studied Scoop then gave a little meh movement of her head. "Maybe."

"And that's why he ended up in Warm Springs. He was looking for the man who conned you on a horse trade."

"I wouldn't know anything about that."

"Then why did you lend him your car? And why did you decide to return to New York for a very important appointment by traveling so far out of your way?"

Stella slammed back her chair and started pacing again. "All right! He was trying to find the little weasel. I wanted my money."

"The little weasel being Curtis Arthur D'Amboise."

"That's not the name he used but, yeah. Tony found out that he'd been going on about being a long-lost descendant of Franklin Roosevelt's. Something about his time in Florida on the Larooco houseboat soon after he contracted polio."

"How did Rousso know he was in Warm Springs?"

"Don't ask me. That's why I hired him. Because he knows how to find things."

The police chief looked at a report in the file on the table. "You've been here for three days."

"At the Lodge."

"Why?"

"Because Tony said he'd found the weasel."

"And what did Tony have to say when you arrived?"

"Nothing. I couldn't find him. He stopped answering his phone. Then the news people started checking into the Lodge, talking about dead bodies. I decided Tony had skipped."

"Did you think he was responsible for the death of D'Amboise?"

"I don't know. Maybe. He's been known to rough people up on occasion. You know, convince them to act in their own best interest."

"In other words, extort money."

"Not on my behalf. I just wanted to find the weasel and get *my* money back. It's not extortion if it's your money."

"When was the last time you saw D'Amboise?"

"Three months ago."

"Rousso has been looking for him for three months?"

"No. I just hired him two weeks ago."

"Why now?"

She shrugged and paced.

The chief pushed back his chair and stood. "I suggest, Ms. Abromowitz, that you cancel your appointment in New York. And don't even think about leaving the jurisdiction."

"You can't do that! I haven't broken any laws."

"I could arrest you as an accessory to murder. Extortion. Impeding a police investigation. Or you can continue to stay in the comfort of the Lodge until we have better answers to our questions. Your choice."

Stella snatched up her fringed leather handbag. "Can I go now?"

"Don't leave Pine Mountain."

Chapter Twenty-Five

The museum grounds are practically deserted. Since the discovery of the murder weapon, there's been only a half-hearted attempt to find the scene of the crime. I can't say that I blame them. It could be anywhere and not necessarily on the compound.

Hannah has taken Teagan to Callaway for a round of golf with her friends. McFadden left some time ago; I assume to do whatever it is you do with a fingerprint. Scoop hasn't yet returned from Pine Mountain.

What's a cat to do?

I suppose I'll just have to hoof it back to the heart of town. Though Teagan shared some of her sandwich with me earlier, I find I'm feeling a little cranky from hunger. It'll soon be time for tea. I think I'll just take myself off to the library. Lil will probably have scones. She's been reading a lot of British cozies lately.

A cool breeze stirs the leaves as I make my way along Highway 27. As I come around the curve, I can see the traffic light in the distance. A police car comes speeding from behind me. It doesn't even slow down for the railroad tracks or the light as it barrels through the heart of Warm Springs. Luckily, the light is green. Lucky for Clay, the train isn't coming. Lucky for the good citizens of Warm Springs no one was attempting to cross Main Street.

I wonder who put a bee in his bonnet?

Lil opens the door when I call out. She's good about that. The library is empty of patrons. I smell the faint scent of tea and lemon and the tantalizing aroma of blueberry. She has made my favorite. As we enjoy the delicious scones, she brings me up to date on the latest happenings of the town.

The Farmer broke the drive shaft on the tractor and can't find a replacement. They've used the library's computer to search online but his tractor is so old that they'll be lucky if they get any responses to his ad on eBay. Harriett gave her granddaughter a perm and the results were less than satisfactory. Now the granddaughter is vowing not to go to the prom. Charlene hasn't shown up for her job at The Bulloch House for the past three days and the owner is threatening to fire her. Lil is afraid she might have run off to Nashville.

The phone rings and Lil goes to answer it. I finish the last of my scone and make my way to the door.

When she's done on the phone, Lil comes to find me. "No nap in the window seat today?"

As tempting as that sounds, I feel the pressure of time. Which is strange for me. In the past I've always considered that a human preoccupation. But there is a killer among us and, much as I hate to admit it, I've become quite fond of Hannah and Teagan. I worry that something will happen to them if I don't find the murderer. And soon.

"Suit yourself," *Lil says as she holds the door open.*

The town is quiet. I wish I knew where to look and what to look for. In the absence of any direction, I think I'll check out The Punk's room again. I doubt there's anything there. Aside from the slip-up with the walking cane, Birdie and McFadden are very proficient at their jobs.

I find the doors to both the hotel and the Tuscawilla Ice Cream Shop closed. I walk along the side porch to the back entrance. It, too, is firmly secure. All my efforts at moving the case along seem to be running into a brick wall. I look across the parking lot at the inviting shade of the swing beneath the arbor by the potting shed. The day is hot. My tummy is full. The swing cushion beckons. I yawn.

Perhaps, in the cause of justice, I should take advantage of this lull in the action and refresh myself. A rested brain is a sharp brain. I don't know who said that. Probably nobody. But I'm sure it must be true.

I cross over to the arbor and hop onto the seat of the swing. I find just the right position on the cushion and close my eyes.

* * *

When Scoop arrived back at the museum, he discovered everyone gone except Oscar, who was working on the daily Wordle puzzle. Even the encampment of photographers and reporters had dwindled to a couple of hardy souls. All the action was probably in the bar at the Callaway Lodge, he decided. The good citizens of Warm Springs had proven to be surprisingly tight lipped about the happenings at the museum and the news hounds were searching for greener pastures in Pine Mountain. Perhaps Teagan was right. They all wanted to protect the reputation of the President.

He thought about checking in at the situation room at the police station but decided he needed the quiet of the empty museum in which to review the files on the case.

He got the wi-fi password from Oscar and put on a fresh pot of coffee. His laptop hummed to life and he began to open files.

No fingerprints had been found on the walking stick which was no surprise. Someone smart enough to set the stage with the clues would be sure nothing incriminating was left behind. The blood embedded in the crevices of the letters on the cane belonged to D'Amboise and the coroner had matched the weapon to the wound.

The same was true of the scythe. Rousso had been struck from behind with the back end of the instrument. The angle of the blow suggested the killer was several inches taller than the victim. That would apply to D'Amboise. It would also apply to Stella Abromowitz.

The fingerprint from the display cabinet was only a partial. An electric cord stapled to the facing of the cabinet ran through the center of the print. Vital elements of the swirls were missing. Nevertheless, they had run it through AFIS in the hope of finding near matches. No luck. The FBI lab was having a look to see if one of their techniques could in some way enhance the image.

The fabric found snagged on the clapboard of the servants' quarters was manufactured in Vietnam. It came in four colors and had been imported by a company out of Atlanta for use in uniforms for various businesses. A list was provided. On the list of customers was the Atlanta Police Department, several county sheriff's departments, and the State of Georgia Parks system. Also listed were about a half dozen private companies within a fifty-mile radius of Warm Springs. The CIRT office in Atlanta had an agent running down customers who purchased uniforms made from the fabric.

That covered the physical evidence. Hopefully one of those avenues would lead to a suspect. In the meantime, he needed to decide what, if anything, in all the interviews and data that had been gathered by the Warm Springs police, the CIRT team, and the FBI, would lead to their man. Or woman.

After an hour and a half and most of the pot of coffee, Scoop had three potential scenarios.

First, and most obvious, was that Rousso had confronted D'Amboise. The coroner had established that he was the first victim. Caught in a tight spot, D'Amboise had lured him to a meeting at Dowdell's Knob and bashed him in the head with the scythe, a weapon that he knew would lead authorities back to the museum. Why? Scoop wondered.

Would Stella Abromowitz have killed Rousso? She could probably have physically pulled it off. But, why? She wouldn't get her money back if he was dead.

No one else had a motive to kill Rousso as far as Scoop could see.

The likelihood of Abromowitz killing D'Amboise didn't fit the circumstances. Whoever whacked him over the head with the cane not only had access to the main building of the museum but also knew where to find the keys to open the protective barrier in the servants' quarters.

The second scenario was that D'Amboise was working a scam to fleece a member of the Roosevelt family or the museum by claiming some entitlement as a descendant. Would a local care enough about the reputation of the family to commit murder? Was the body dump intended to send a message against such schemes?

Or, as a third scenario, had another of D'Amboise's

con victims caught up with him? Was the location of the museum for the body dump simply a misdirection? That led right back to the problem of access to plant the weapon and the body.

As he was pondering these possibilities, Scoop's phone vibrated and he looked down at the number. "Clay, what's going on?" he asked.

"We have another body."

* * *

The Girls arranged to meet Hannah and Teagan at the Big Top parking lot in two golf carts.

"You wouldn't believe it," Phyllis said, "the place is overflowing with reporters and camera men. Good thing for us none of them are here to play golf. We should pretty much have the links to ourselves. At this hour, all the serious golfers have retired to the bar."

"I resent that remark," Jackie said. "*We* are serious golfers."

Everyone laughed.

"Well," Hannah said, "at least we'll have fun and we won't be rushed by a line of players wanting to play through."

"I propose we head to LaGrange afterwards," Sue said. "I met a woman in the spa this morning who raved about a new restaurant called Mama Mia's. A little Italian pasta after nine holes will suit me down to the ground."

"What about Fergus?" Teagan asked.

Sue smiled and bent down to give Fergus a scratch behind his ears. "They have *al fresco* dining. Fergus will fit right in."

Teagan had been reluctant to leave the museum for this excursion. Hannah knew she wanted to be there in case Scoop or McFadden returned. The investigation was the only thing on her mind.

"Come on," she said. "Let's see who has to pay for dinner."

With happy banter about prowess and luck, the women climbed into the golf carts with Fergus riding shotgun in Sue and Teagan's cart. Hannah could only hope that once they got involved in the game, Teagan would forget about the investigation. She was a very good golfer and took the game seriously.

As they set off on the twisting lane toward their first tee, Hannah saw a Warm Springs patrol car pull into the parking lot. The vehicle was too far away for her to determine who the driver was. What was a Warm Springs patrolman doing in Pine Mountain? Did Clay have someone watching after them? A shiver ran down her spine.

Chapter Twenty-Six

I awaken to the sound of car doors slamming. With a yawn I see that Birdie has arrived at the bed and breakfast. I hope her mission with the walking cane was successful. I stretch and wander over to see what's what.

"Hello, Callahan. Good to see a friendly face," *she says.*

I wonder if the people in Atlanta were unkind to her. Surely not. Birdie is a most agreeable human.

"I'm starving. What's for dinner?"

I look at her. This can't be a serious question. Perhaps this is human humor.

She takes her case out of the trunk of the automobile that has delivered her and shakes hands with the driver.

I follow as she climbs the steps to the rear entrance of the hotel and opens the door. We climb the stairs to the third floor and she deposits her bag on the bed as she slips off her shoes.

"What a day," *she says as she proceeds to wash her hands and face in the tiny sink in the corner of the room.* "The FBI lab is awesome."

I assume no comment is expected on my part and I hop onto the bed and listen as she rattles off all the wonders of this establishment. None of it makes sense to me but she is clearly enthralled. If Scoop isn't careful, I fear his favorite investigator might be lured from the ranks of his team by the charms of this newfound wonder.

Just as Birdie stretches out on the bed with a sigh, her phone vibrates.

"Crap."

She taps the screen, looks at it a moment, then jumps from the bed. Suddenly she is all motion. Her shoes are back on in a flash, she runs a brush through her hair, and she has her bag in hand and headed out the door in two shakes of a cat's tail.

* * *

The Red Oak Creek covered bridge was seventeen miles from Warm Springs. Scoop took Hwy 27 through the heart of town to Georgia State 85 where he floored it. When he arrived outside Woodbury fifteen minutes later, he found two Meriwether County Sheriff's cars and Billy Brad's patrol car on the scene.

Billy Brad looked ashen when Scoop approached the entrance to the bridge.

"It's Charlene."

Scoop searched his memory for the name. The waitress from The Bulloch House.

"How'd she die?"

"Struck on the side of the head at the temple. Don't

know what was used."

Scoop studied the patrolman's face. "You okay?"

He shook his head. "Not really. I've known Charlene all her life." He swallowed. "This is going to kill her mama."

Was this related to the two other murders? All had occurred at historic sites, though the bridge had no specific tie to Roosevelt that Scoop was aware of.

"Anything stand out to you? Anything that doesn't belong at the scene?"

But Billy Brad couldn't seem to focus. "I don't know," he said. He kept staring down the length of the bridge at the figures midway across, carefully working their way out from the body inch by inch. "I don't know."

The bright light coming through the other end of the bridge made it hard to tell what the deputies were doing but Scoop knew. So did Billy Brad. If there were any clues, they would find them.

"What was she doing out here?"

Billy Brad shrugged and gave a small shake of his head.

Then it came to him. Scoop remembered what the waitress at The Bulloch House had said about Charlene's singing. That she liked to perform all over the county and post those videos to TikTok.

"Did you find her guitar?"

"What?"

"The guitar. Did she have it with her?"

"No. At least it isn't here now."

But she had a guitar. The video from the SD card they found in D'Amboise's room had shown a clip of her performing at this very spot. The guitar she was strumming had a bright blue pick guard against the burled wood body.

"How did she get here?"

"Don't know. But she was killed here. Right where she is."

Scoop looked around the sandy soil that accommodated parking for people who came to tour the bridge. There were tire tracks and footprints everywhere, even down the slope to the water's edge.

His phone vibrated. Birdie and McFadden were on their way. Scoop glanced anxiously at the horizon. The sun was getting low in the sky. They wouldn't have much daylight left.

* * *

After The Girls got into the flow of the game of golf, Teagan appeared to have put the murder investigation out of her mind. The trip to LaGrange for dinner proved to be a success. Everyone was in high spirits and they lingered over their meal, finishing it off with tiramisu for dessert.

By the time Hannah pulled into their driveway it was very late. Teagan was asleep in the passenger seat. There had been no mention of the case all evening. For that, Hannah was thankful. The floodlights were a welcome sight when she pulled into the carport. With a sigh, she turned off the car and gave Teagan a gentle shake. Fergus roused himself and yawned. They were all tired.

For once, there was no resistance to bedtime. Hannah tucked Teagan in tight. Fergus settled beside her bed. Hannah made her way to the kitchen for a glass of water. Clouds were drifting across the moon as she watched from the kitchen window. With a yawn, she plugged her phone into the charger and began to scroll through messages before calling it a night.

Once again, she discovered dozens of emails. She scrolled through most of them, checking an occasional one from a friend or co-worker. Nothing that couldn't wait. Just as she was about to close her phone a text popped up. *Is this David Sanderson's widow?*

Hannah felt the blood drain from her head. She grabbed the edge of the sink to steady herself. The number for the message was blocked. Suddenly, the power went off, throwing the room into darkness. The half-moon had disappeared behind a bank of clouds. In the absence of the outdoor lights, the landscape was pitch black.

Chapter Twenty-Seven

Everyone is going about their tasks in a very solemn manner. And rightly so. Charlene was a beautiful young woman. I remember her now. Had she been part of the kitchen staff at The Bulloch House I'm sure I would have remembered her immediately. I now realize she was the one trying to pick the lock on D'Amboise's room two days ago. Perhaps the reason I failed to recognize her is because she wasn't in her usual garb or her usual environment.

They say she had a lovely voice. I suppose that's true. Music for humans is a desired thing. They find it enjoyable. But then, they don't have my sensitive hearing. Her dreams of becoming a country music star will never happen now. What a pity.

Who would have done such a wicked thing?

It can't be blamed on D'Amboise. I recall having seen him hanging about Eleanor's Alley where Charlene would show up and they'd put their heads together. At the time it hadn't made much of an impression, just the usual hanky-panky. A lot of the young people in town find it a convenient and semi-private meeting up spot. It does lend itself to secret assignations. And Alice's fancy man could be a charmer when he needed to be. That Punk!

There must be some connection between Charlene's death and the other murders. After all, she was looking for something in D'Amboise's room. This is something Scoop and the team should know. How to communicate this to him is another matter. I don't see how it can be done. And I'm a clever cat.

Clay arrives on the scene. He gives me a look then turns to Scoop. "Find anything?" *he asks.*

Scoop stops scrolling through messages on his phone. His forehead creases as he gives Clay a squinty eyed look.

"I was over at Pine Mountain. No cell reception. Just got the call from Patti. I can't believe it." *Clay gives a slow shake of his head.* "Jeez. Three bodies. What the devil is going on?"

"How well did D'Amboise know Charlene?"

"Beats me. Well enough, I imagine. We know he recorded her singing at The Bulloch House."

"And right here."

Clay cuts his eyes at Scoop then away. "Yeah."

They stand in silence for a moment as they watch the men combing the banks of the creek.

Clay clears his throat. "I should go tell her mama. I wouldn't want her to hear it from anyone else."

Scoop doesn't answer immediately. Finally, he says, "You do that. We'll be here a while."

Scoop isn't happy about something. Well, other than the fact that his case has suddenly been complicated by another body. Something is bothering him.

* * *

Scoop let the hot shower wash away the grit and images of the afternoon. They had worked into the night with the aid of portable lighting. Nothing of value had been recovered from the scene.

He had gone with Billy Brad afterward to comfort Charlene's mother. It was important to speak with her himself. He needed to get what information they could about Charlene's activities over the last few days. He had found Clay's notes on the D'Amboise case rather light. The stakes were mounting. They needed to be thorough. Besides, Scoop liked to hear the facts first hand. What was said, and what wasn't.

Something had happened, her mother said. She didn't know what, only that Charlene was worried, preoccupied. The restaurant had called twice because she didn't show up for her shift. Her mother hadn't been able to get anything out of Charlene about why.

The only thing they learned was that Charlene hadn't been dating anyone in particular. She would go out occasionally but mostly on her own to events where her friends would gather. She hadn't wanted any attachments for fear it would derail her ambition to head out to Nashville in the fall.

When asked, her mother had gone in search of Charlene's guitar. It wasn't anywhere to be found.

Where did that leave them, Scoop wondered, as he shut off the water and stepped out of the shower. Nowhere. No motive, no weapon, no clues.

He was about to crawl between the sheets when his phone rang. It was nearly midnight. It was Hannah Sanderson.

* * *

"I'm sorry," Hannah said the moment Scoop answered his phone. "I—I know it's late but—"

"What is it? Are you and Teagan all right?"

"Yes." She sighed. "No. Not really. This is going to sound silly, but—"

"Tell me."

"The lights went out."

There was a brief silence. "And."

"Something about it doesn't feel right. Like when we came home to find the door to the house open."

"I'm on my way."

"No, don't—"

"Ten minutes. Is Teagan asleep?"

"Yes."

"Don't wake her. Stay in the room with her and Fergus. Lock the bedroom door. I'll flash my headlights when I get there."

With that, Scoop ended the connection.

Hannah felt foolish for having called, but she was glad she did. His instructions to stay in Teagan's room behind a locked door only spooked her more. A sense of doom had followed her like a dark shadow since the discovery of D'Amboise's body. Try as she might, she had been unable to shake it. Each new misadventure only added to the darkness.

Initially she had felt removed from the murder. As awful as it was, it seemed unrelated to her or Teagan except for the concern that it would somehow reignite the anxiety Teagan had experienced with her father's death. All that had changed when Hannah discovered the open door to their sanctuary. It was as though wickedness was seeping into every corner of their lives.

She shivered. She was glad Scoop was coming over. He made her feel safe. She missed that feeling. David had made her feel that way. But David hadn't been around much in the last two years of their marriage. And when he was, he had been a different person. The world was a different place. Even in this remote rural corner of southwest Georgia.

True to his word, in less than ten minutes she saw the flash of his headlights. She eased out of Teagan's room and closed the door behind her. When Scoop tapped gently on the glass of the door pane, Hannah used the light of her cell phone to be sure that it was him even though she knew that it was. She was that spooked.

She opened the door and he stepped in and wrapped her in his arms. They stood there in the dark for a long moment and she let herself be comforted by his warmth.

"Are you okay?" he asked quietly.

She nodded, then reluctantly pulled back from his embrace. "I feel rather foolish."

"Don't. I'm going to check the premises and see if there's anything to be concerned about. But first let's check your power box."

"The breaker is here in the pantry but none of the switches are thrown. The main feed is behind the house near the far corner."

Scoop had a flashlight with him. He threw all the switches in the breaker box to be sure the problem wasn't there. "Do you have any candles?"

"Yes."

"Let's get them. I'm going outside and I don't want you sitting here in the dark."

Hannah lifted a box down from the top pantry shelf while Scoop held the flashlight. They took it to the living room and lit three of the big fat Christmas candles.

"Don't move from this room while I'm outside."

His words chilled her. Did he think someone had been out there? That they could still be out there?

Hannah drew her feet up onto the couch and hugged herself as she sat waiting. It seemed Scoop was gone a long time. She began to think something had happened to him. Had he left the door unlocked when he went outside? Her heart was racing when she heard a soft sound in the kitchen.

Scoop appeared in the candlelit doorway of the living room and Hannah gave a little squeak.

"Sorry," he said as he crossed the room to sit beside her on the sofa. He put his arm around her shoulders. "There's a problem with the feed line. We'll get it looked at tomorrow. I'm afraid we'll be in the dark until then."

Hannah relaxed against him, her heart rate slowly returning to normal. "Thank you for coming. I'm afraid I let my imagination run away with me. You must be dead tired. You should go."

"It's late. If it's okay with you, I'll crash here on the sofa."

"You don't have to do that. Honest. Now that I know it's just an electrical short, I'll be fine." She pulled back a little and studied his face in the candlelight. "You've had a long day, haven't you?"

"Yes." He surprised her by kissing her on the forehead. "So, if you have a spare pillow—"

"Of course." Hannah felt her heart flutter. "I'll be right back."

Once she had Scoop settled on the sofa, she took one of the candles to her room. She read the text message again. It had been on the tip of her tongue to confide in him about it. The lines of fatigue and worry on his face had changed her mind. She would speak to him about it in the morning when everything would be better with the bright light of a new day. When he was rested.

Chapter Twenty-Eight

Birdie is a restless sleeper. She tosses and turns and talks in her sleep. Had I known this I would have opted for the swing in the arbor. Or the rocking chair on the porch of The Country Classics Boutique. From there, I would have a view of all of Broad Street. Not that I plan to be doing much looking. Just like Birdie, I'm beat.

I guess I'm turning into what they call a soft touch. She seemed so down. The lack of progress on the case and now a third death has the whole crew feeling guilty. I don't quite understand how that came to pass. It isn't as if they had anything to do with any of the deaths. Human guilt is a strange thing to get a handle on and there seems to be a wide variety. Catholic guilt, Jewish mothers' guilt, survivor's guilt. The list goes on. I'm fortunate to be a cat. I'll leave it for others to wrestle with this phenomenon. Now I sit here in the window overlooking downtown Warm Springs. It's so quiet and peaceful.

How did all this mayhem befall such a quaint little place?

The why I'll leave to others as well, but the who, that's another matter. I'm ready to find this villain and deal with him. How to go about doing so is the question.

A patrol car crawls along Broad Street, keeping a watchful eye on the citizens as they sleep. If only it was that simple.

I hop back onto the bed with Birdie and nestle against her back. She mumbles and after a bit settles into restful sleep. I yawn and close my eyes. We're both going to need our wits about us come the morning. There's so much to do.

* * *

Scoop opened his eyes to the sound of Fergus panting near his ear. The dog was watching him, his tongue lolling out of his mouth. Teagan was watching him, too.

"Good morning," he said.

"What are you doing on the couch?" Teagan had a very serious look on her face.

"The lights went out last night. I came to check the fuse. It was too late to go back to the hotel."

"Why?"

"Because the outside door is locked at that hour and I would have had to wake Alice."

He watched as Teagan considered his answer for a moment. Apparently, she was satisfied with it.

"Are you hungry?" she asked.

"I'm always hungry."

"Fergus is too."

Scoop glanced at the window. It was still very early. "Where's your mother?"

"Still asleep. I'll go wake her."

"Why don't we let her sleep a little longer. It's Saturday. And, she was up late last night."

"We went to LaGrange."

"Yeah? What did you do in LaGrange?"

"Ate at the Italian restaurant."

"Was it good?"

Teagan didn't answer his question. Instead she said, "A police car followed us."

"To LaGrange?"

She nodded.

"What did your mother think about that?"

"She didn't see it."

"I expect Clay had someone watching out for the two of you."

"Like a stakeout?"

"Something like that."

"Why?"

Scoop shrugged. "I think he wants to keep a watchful eye on you."

"Because of the murders?"

"Yes." Scoop fell silent for a moment. "And because he likes your mother."

Teagan made a face.

Scoop smiled. He was inclined to agree with her on that one. "Did you see the car when you came home?"

Teagan shook her head. "He was parked on the other side of the square from the restaurant for a while. We ate outside. It's called *al fresco*."

"Is it?"

She nodded. "Then he left."

Fergus gave a soft whine and headed toward the door. He stopped and looked back at them.

"He needs to go out." With that, Teagan followed after him.

Scoop heard the back door open and close. He checked his phone for messages as he went to stand by the window and watch Teagan and Fergus in the yard. He had responses to his late-night texts from both Birdie and McFadden. They knew where he was and the circumstances. He needed to tell Hannah before they arrived.

He hadn't had the heart to tell her last night.

* * *

Hannah woke to the murmur of voices. She lay in bed listening to the sound of Teagan and Scoop. It was a comforting sound. She stretched, then rolled out of bed. Her hair was all over the place so she dashed the brush through it a couple of times then slipped into the bathroom to brush her teeth.

She found Scoop standing at the window, looking out, his back to her, the phone to his ear.

"Twenty minutes," he said, then ended the call.

"Good morning."

He turned at the sound of her voice.

"Good morning. Did you sleep?"

"Surprisingly, I did. And soundly, too."

"Good. You needed the rest."

"So did you." But she could tell that he hadn't rested very well. "Sorry about the sofa."

"It's not the sofa." He guided her to an armchair. "We need to talk."

Hannah was suddenly wary. "What?"

"There's been another murder."

She drew a sharp breath. "Oh, my God. Who?"

"Charlene."

"What!"

"At the Red Oak Creek bridge. Sometime after noon yesterday."

"You knew this last night?"

"Yes."

"Why didn't you tell me?"

"You were upset and frightened. I knew it would only add to your distress."

Hannah braced her elbows on her knees and lowered her face into her hands. "What is happening!"

Scoop knelt beside her chair. "I want you and Teagan to go stay with your friends at the Lodge until this is over. I've arranged accommodations. You'll have an escort there so you can have your car handy. But, Hannah, pay attention to my words."

Her hands dropped away from her face and she stared into Scoop's eyes.

"Do not go off on your own. Remain with your friends. Keep Teagan close."

"You're scaring me," she said in a hushed voice. "What aren't you telling me?"

He took her hands in his. "Last night's power failure wasn't an accident. Someone cut the powerline."

Hannah surged to her feet and Scoop caught her in his arms, holding her close as she struggled to break free.

"Listen to me, Hannah. I'll find him. I promise you. I'll find him and he will pay, but I need to know that you and Teagan are safe."

She stopped resisting and rested her forehead against his chest.

He lifted her chin, brushed her hair back then kissed her, long and deep.

The sound of the kitchen door closing broke the spell and he released her.

"Don't alarm Teagan," he said in a low voice. "Make it an adventure. Birdie and McFadden will be here in about twenty minutes to process the scene. It would be a good idea to get Teagan away from here before they arrive."

Hannah paled at his words, nodded, and turned toward the kitchen. Teagan was too curious for her own good. She had to get her away from the house before the CIRT team arrived.

Chapter Twenty-Nine

Breakfast was a very glum affair. Birdie and McFadden had little to say before they loaded up the van and headed out of town, except for an occasional cryptic word or phrase that I suppose all forensic scientists understand. I've no idea what they have on the agenda or where they have gone, but I know what I'll be doing. It's time to tune into the old grapevine. Today Charlene's Mama will receive consolation from her friends and neighbors. Coffee will be consumed, iced tea sipped, and apple pies baked. That's the beauty of a small town.

In that mix there will be words of comfort, advice, and subtle inquiry. They will bless Charlene's Mama's heart and distract her with local gossip. As they sow, so shall they reap. And I will be the wiser for having heard it all. There's the added benefit of all those covered dishes that will burden the kitchen table and overflow the refrigerator. I see good eating for days to come.

Even as I stroll down the crepe myrtle lined driveway a car pulls to a stop out by the mailbox. It's The Preacher's Wife. That'll be pulled pork in the aluminum pan she's carrying, unless I'm sadly mistaken.

"Bless your heart, Barbara Jean. What a sad, sad day." The Preacher's Wife tut-tuts and shakes her head. "Let me put this in the kitchen. Just a little something for when folks stop by. How about I brew you a fresh pot of coffee? Hmmm?"

I follow The Preacher's Wife into the kitchen. Already there's a bowl of something with lightly-toasted meringue spikes peaking above the rim. Seems Jolene over at the beauty parlor has already been and gone. Unfortunate that I missed her, for the beauty parlor is the epicenter of heart blessings and gentle reprimands for the small indiscretions of sleeping in church, sassing your mama, and being a little too attentive to the new secretary at the insurance agent's office.

Charlene's Mama has a good cry, another cup of coffee, and swears she doesn't know where she went wrong in raising that young'un. If only she'd been satisfied to lift her voice to the Lord in the church choir, none of this would be happening. Just hearing the word Nashville sets her off into a gale of tears.

Two more Church Ladies arrive. The kitchen is beginning to smell better than The Bulloch House on a Saturday night. They talk about the hymns Charlene's Mama will want for the service. They give each other a look and a sad shake of the head while Charlene's Mama weeps into her handkerchief. When Charlene's Mama goes to answer a knock at the door, The Church Ladies begin to whisper furiously about Charlene being seen canoodling with that dead man.

Hello. What's this? Someone else knows about the rendezvous in Eleanor's Alley.

But, wait. She was seen having lunch WITH WINE with him at the Lodge.

The Church Ladies fall silent when Charlene's Mama and The Banker enter the kitchen in search of coffee.

A steady stream of people come and go. I find a lot has happened in the community since I've been involved in tracking down murderers. Most of it is irrelevant and sometimes amusing. The arrival of The Preacher moves the conversation to the front porch. He's a kind man but, to be honest, his platitudes cause me to nod off.

When I wake I find myself all alone. The screen door is closed so I head around to the back. From the back porch a hallway leads through the center of the house. When I get about halfway to the parlor I hear a faint noise. The door to the room on the left is slightly ajar. I slip through the opening. Billy Brad is going through a desk placed under a window. From the number of posters of country singers, I deduce that this is Charlene's room.

What's he looking for? Clues, I suppose. Something that will shed some light on who in Charlene's life would want to harm her. If only I could read.

He's being very quiet. Actually, he's being quite secretive if his repeated glances toward the door are anything to go by. He probably doesn't want to upset Charlene's Mama. She has cried buckets this morning. To be reminded of why Billy Brad is searching Charlene's room would, I imagine, be the last straw.

Suddenly, his cell phone makes that buzzing, vibrating sound. He swears softly under his breath as he puts his hand over the device to silence it. After a quick glance at the face of it, he swears again and eases the bedroom door open, looks both ways down the hallway, then hurries quietly out the back door.

There is something not quite right about this behavior. I hop onto the desk and nose around through the odds and ends. I see nothing of interest. As I hop down, I bump the drawer Billy Brad has left open. From the underside a piece of paper dislodges and falls to the floor. I inspect it but find it's only a small rectangle with scribblings on it and a picture of a bus with a long, lean greyhound on the side. There's nothing to see here.

So far, the only thing I've learned during my visit is that Charlene was more involved with D'Amboise than her Mama knew. Which brings us back around to the conclusion that the deaths are related.

* * *

Teagan took the news that they were meeting Sue at The Country Store for breakfast much better than Hannah thought she would. Even the realization they were checking into the Lodge for the rest of the weekend so they wouldn't be running back and forth didn't get a rise out of her. The golf of the previous afternoon and the evening in LaGrange had allowed her to open up more to The Girls. Hannah decided she was enjoying their company.

Scoop followed them to Pine Mountain. Knowing how observant Teagan was, he made a point, before they set out from the house, to tell them he had to meet with the Pine Mountain police chief.

Hannah would have to find an occasion to bring her friends into the picture so they could all be vigilant. She hadn't had the opportunity to tell Scoop about the text message she'd received just before the lights went out the previous evening. He had enough on his hands, she decided. It could wait. She worried that it was a reporter and he might be staying at the Lodge. Her other worry was that he wasn't a reporter. There was no question in her mind that someone was stalking her and Teagan. Someone who meant them greater harm than exposing their identities.

Sue was waiting for them when they arrived at the restaurant. The Country Store was known for its homestyle meals. Teagan ate well, slipping bits of biscuit under the table to Fergus. The sunlight poured through the windows behind her, turning her blonde hair to spun gold. She threw back her head to laugh at something Sue said.

The image struck a chord with Hannah. A kind of *deja vu* moment. She remembered seeing Charlene sitting at this very table singing for one of her TikTok videos. Something else about that day teased at the edge of memory but she couldn't retrieve it.

How her mother must be hurting, Hannah thought. And how thankful she was that she and Teagan were here, safe from harm. She didn't want to think what might have happened if Scoop hadn't reached them so quickly the night before. Would the stalker have made his move? Or was he content to terrorize her?

* * *

Once Hannah and Teagan were safely with Sue, Scoop returned to Warm Springs and the incident room at the police station. He and the team needed a brainstorming session to re-sift the facts, find a different perspective on how they all fit together.

Birdie and McFadden found nothing useful at Hannah's house. McFadden took a portion from both ends of the cut powerline with the view to potentially matching it to the cutting tool. A long shot for sure, but they had nothing else to go on. No footprints around the house, no fingerprints other than Scoop's.

They were working their way through a pot of coffee and a pile of interviews the Warm Springs police department had conducted.

"Bingo," Birdie said.

"What?"

"Sheila Morris saw Charlene with D'Amboise in Eleanor's Alley last Sunday. They were deep in conversation and Charlene gave her a 'look' when she slowed at the mouth of the alley to see what they were up to."

"D'Amboise isn't the only one." McFadden got up and closed the door. "A kid that works at the service station said he saw Clay giving Charlene a hard time in the parking lot of the Dollar General. He couldn't hear what they were arguing about but it got heated."

The door of the incident room opened and Clay walked in. He looked from Scoop to McFadden, then Birdie. "What's going on?"

"Trying to get a picture of Charlene. What she was like," Scoop said.

"She was a good girl." Clay's voice held a defensive note. "She argued with her mother about going to Nashville but that was just her trying to grow up, to follow her dream. There was no meanness to it."

"What about everyone else around town? Did she get along with folks generally?"

"Sure."

"Ever know her to have a falling out with anyone?"

"Charlene? Heck, no. She was happy. Always singing. Entertained the folks with *Happy Birthday*, stuff like that, over at the restaurant. She was just—" he gave a gentle shake of his head. "She was just happy."

McFadden started to speak but a slight movement of Scoop's hand made him hold his tongue.

"I didn't see you when I got here this morning." Scoop leaned back in his chair and clicked a pen open, closed, open, closed as he watched Clay.

"I was on a call. Other things than murder do happen around here, you know." There was a slight defensive note in his voice. He looked over at McFadden. "I swung by Hannah's. She wasn't home. Not at the museum either. What'd you find at her place?"

Scoop gave the barest of nods.

McFadden shrugged. "Nothing."

"Know where she is?"

"Not a clue."

"Right." Clay cleared his throat. "Got this from Pine Mountain." He dropped a file onto the table. "The FBI lab lifted a print on the scythe. It belongs to D'Amboise."

"Then we were right. D'Amboise lured Rousso somewhere and bashed his skull in. Whether or not Stella Abromowitz is involved remains to be seen. Now all we need to do is figure out who killed D'Amboise."

"And Charlene," Birdie said.

"And Charlene," Scoop replied.

As soon as Clay closed the door behind him, Scoop turned to McFadden and Birdie. "Who told him about the problem at Hannah's?"

Birdie and McFadden looked at each other then back at Scoop and shook their heads.

"No one," McFadden said.

"So how did he know? Did you tell anyone else?"

Again, they both shook their heads.

"You said to keep it quiet so it wouldn't get back to Teagan so we didn't mention it."

Scoop rose from the chair and moved to the window overlooking the street. He saw Clay exit the police station, get into his patrol car, and drive away.

Where was he going? Scoop wondered.

"Does anyone other than the three of us know that Hannah and Teagan are at Callaway?"

Birdie came to stand beside him at the window. The street was quiet. "We haven't told anyone."

Would Hannah have told the local police department? Scoop didn't think so.

"I don't like it."

"Neither do I," Birdie said.

Scoop took out his phone and dialed Hannah's number. It rang and rang before going to voice mail.

"I really don't like it," Scoop said under his breath as he crossed the room and out the door toward his car.

McFadden ran after him. "Boss! What should we do?"

Scoop stopped, his car door open, one foot already inside. "Find me something in those reports. Something to connect Clay to Charlene. She's the key. She's the reason for all of it."

He got into the car and tore away from the station down Highway 27.

Chapter Thirty

I now know why they call it comfort food. Too much of several good things has me feeling quite sleepy and content. Perhaps the walk to the hotel will clear my head.

I can't say that I learned much that was useful to the case this morning, but it was necessary. You never know when an innocent statement will be the clue that leads right to the open window on a rainy night. Or, in this case, to the murderer. No such luck today but at least I've eliminated The Preacher, The Banker, The Church Ladies, and The Farmer's Wife. Not that I thought it was any of them, but they must be scratched off the list in order to move forward.

The train has slowed to a crawl as it eases through town. Since the hotel is on the other side of the tracks, I'll just pop in and see how Trudy is doing at the Tourist Information Center.

But, what's this?

Billy Brad and Clay are having a heated conversation, if body language is anything to go by. And right here in the parking lot of the Tourist Center. I can't make out what they're saying because of the creaking and screeching of the train so I'll just get a little closer…

"I don't care," *Clay is red in the face,* "just keep your mouth shut!"

"It was a dumb idea."

"You let me worry about that. I mean it, Billy Brad. Get rid of it. Now!" *Clay turns and stalks off across the railroad tracks just as the caboose rumbles past.*

"Fine!" *Billy Brad shouts after him. The look on his face is one of pure malice as he watches Clay get into his patrol car and drive away with a squeal of tires.*

If looks could kill.

Billy Brad moves to the rear of his own patrol car, stands there and looks around for a minute, then opens the trunk.

I'm a little too far away to see what's inside but if what I can see is what I think it is, then we have a big problem. The hair on my back stands up and I dash across the tracks in search of Scoop.

* * *

Hannah sat in a lounger by the pool while Teagan played Marco Polo with some kids. She had one of Jackie's beach reads open before her but behind her dark glasses, she monitored everyone who came and went around them.

Phyllis came walking toward her with a frou-frou drink with little umbrellas in each hand. As she got near she began to chant, "Mai tai, semper fi, who *is* that good looking guy!"

Hannah laughed. It was the sing-song teasing of their last year at college when she had first met David. It was a happy memory, one that brought a smile to her face.

"So," Phyllis said as she settled onto the seat beside Hannah, "have a little sip and spill the beans. Will Scoop be hanging around after all this messy business is over?"

Hannah laughed again. "I very much doubt it. The best I can hope for is that life will return to normal and we'll be no worse for the wear."

Phyllis studied her friend for a moment. "I don't believe a word of it."

"Well, you should. I'm pretty sure Scoop Russell can't wait to see the back of Warm Springs and all of us."

"Hmmm." Phyllis took a sip of her drink. "Then why is he making a bee line to you as we speak?"

Hannah turned and saw that Phyllis was right. Scoop's long stride had him standing over her before she could take in the fact that he was there, at the Lodge, and apparently, intent on speaking with her.

"If you'll excuse me," Phyllis said as she gracefully stood, "I think I need to refresh my drink." With that she gave Hannah a wink and walked away in the direction of the bar with a little more sway to her hips.

Scoop took the seat Phyllis had vacated and scanned the pool until he spied Teagan. Then he turned to Hannah. "Tell me about Clay."

"Clay? What about him?"

"Anything. Everything. How long have you known him?"

"Since I moved here. Two years now."

"How well do you know him?"

Hannah frowned. "Why all these questions about Clay?"

"Do you date? Is it serious?"

"Date? Clay?" Hannah stared at him. "No."

"But he would like to go out with you, right?"

Hannah felt the blush rising.

"Has he ever been aggressive? Ever made you feel uncomfortable? Threatened?"

"Clay? Of course not." She looked away from his relentless scrutiny. "Okay. He's been trying to get me to go out with him for a while. He's a nice guy. A flirt. All the single women around here enjoy his flirting. And his company."

"But not you."

"I haven't wanted to date anyone. He knows that."

"Does he?"

"Yes."

"Did he date Charlene?"

"Charlene? No." She frowned. "I don't think so. She's so young. Much too young for Clay."

Hannah suddenly realized that Scoop wasn't asking questions about Clay because he thought she had an interest in him. He was asking for a much different reason. "You don't think—can't think that Clay—" She stared at Scoop. "What do you think?"

"I don't know but there's a connection. Charlene is the key. Her death had something to do with everything that's happened. Except for Rousso. We're fairly confident D'Amboise killed Rousso over something that happened before he came to Warm Springs. But Charlene was killed because she was involved somehow with D'Amboise. With his death. Or she knew who was."

"What makes you think that?"

"A gut feeling. I don't know the why. Yet."

"You think he's the killer, don't you?"

Scoop took her hand in his. "I have no motive. I have no physical evidence." He rubbed his thumb along the back of her hand. "Maybe I'm just not seeing things clearly."

"But something makes you suspicious of him."

"Little things. He's never where he should be. He knows things he shouldn't."

"It's a small town."

"True. Just keep in mind my suspicions, will you?"

"Of course."

He gave her hand a squeeze then released it. "I have to go."

Hannah watched until he disappeared through the door into the Lodge. Could he be right about Clay? No. Surely not. Clay was one of the good guys even if he was a notorious flirt. She realized it was probably Clay who had been watching over her and Teagan. It must have been him in the police car at the golf course. That was why Scoop felt he was never where he should be.

* * *

Scoop had been reluctant to alarm Hannah with his suspicions but he felt it was necessary to keep her safe. Clay's interest in her had been obvious from their first encounter. Was he allowing his own feelings to cloud his judgment? Maybe. But someone was keeping close tabs on Hannah. Someone in the Warm Springs police department. Was it for the sake of her safety or for some more sinister reason?

He pulled into the police station parking lot and found Callahan pacing back and forth in front of the door. As Scoop approached the cat began to complain loudly, something that he hadn't done before.

"Go on," Scoop said. "I don't have anything to eat."

His comment only made the cat's protest even louder. The moment Scoop opened the door, Callahan hurried in and went straight to the situation room.

"Boss," Birdie said, "I think I found something." She handed him two sheets. One was the police interview of Joyce Favor. The other, the interview of Jolene, the beautician.

Scoop read through both of them quickly. He saw that Clay was the officer who had taken Jolene's statement.

"Did Clay mention this to either of you?"

"No."

The cat jumped up onto the table and paced the length of it, complaining all the while.

"Give him something to eat, for Christ's sake!" Scoop growled.

But when Birdie placed a cinnamon roll on a napkin for Callahan, he ignored it and continued to complain in a less vocal voice.

"Something's wrong with him," she said.

With that, Callahan stood on his hind legs with his front paws against Birdie's chest. It was as if he was trying to talk to her. "He wants something."

Scoop didn't appear to have heard her. He was staring off into space, the witness statement in his hand. Finally, he said, "We need to question Clay."

"That'll be tricky," McFadden replied.

Scoop dropped the report onto the table. "Where is he now, do we know?"

"I checked as soon as we found this. He called in about fifteen minutes ago. Said he'd be off the clock for lunch for an hour."

"Home?"

"Didn't say."

Scoop considered this a minute. "Mac, you come with me. Birdie, you stay here." Scoop moved toward the door and the cat jumped from the table. "Check the call log. As discreetly as possible. I want to know every move he's made since the discovery of D'Amboise's body."

Chapter Thirty-One

Scoop is so focused that he doesn't see me slip into the car on the passenger side when McFadden opens the door. I can see the hesitation on McFadden's face but in the end, he relents as I slip between the seat and the door frame to the back seat.

We tear out of the parking lot as McFadden rattles off an address. When we reach our destination, Scoop doesn't so much as slow down. There's no sign of the patrol car so there's no reason to stop.

"Where to?" McFadden asks.

Both he and Scoop are scanning up and down the streets as they cruise through town.

After a few minutes of silence, Scoop says, "The bridge."

McFadden opens his window and sticks the blue light on the roof of the car. Scoop guns it as we race along the country roads to the covered bridge, overtaking cars and barely slowing for the small communities we pass through.

As we approach the bridge, he kills the light. A Warm Springs police car is parked on the shoulder of the road leading up to the creek crossing.

Scoop parks strategically behind the car and he and McFadden get out. I slip out with them.

Though they close their doors quietly, Billy Brad is aware of our presence. He's standing a few feet inside the entrance to the bridge, staring down the length of it, the beautiful burled guitar with the bright blue pick guard in his left hand. His revolver in his right.

Scoop and McFadden move their coats to expose their sidearms. Billy Brad turns slowly as they approach. There are tears in his eyes.

"She was going to leave with him." *He looks off to the side as if he's taking in the beauty of the creek one last time.* "He promised her he could make her a star. But it was a lie." *He shakes his head sadly and returns his focus to Scoop.* "She wouldn't believe me. She wanted it so bad."

"This isn't the answer, Billy Brad," *Scoop says in a voice not devoid of kindness.*

"I wanted to marry her. I would have gone to Nashville with her, done whatever she wanted." *A ghost of a smile flits across his features.* "All she wanted was her music."

"Tell me what happened."

"It doesn't matter."

"It matters to her mama."

A pained expression crosses his face. "I'm sorry about that. I didn't mean it to happen. Not to her. But she was scared. She was going to talk. I lost my temper."

The whole time while they're talking, Scoop and McFadden are inching closer.

Billy Brad points his gun at them. "Stay back. It's better this way."

"Death is never the answer," *Scoop tells him.*

I fan out to the far edge of the bridge where the walls of the structure meet the road bed and make my way very slowly forward, easing past Billy Brad.

"I'm a country boy," *Billy Brad says.* "Prison is not for me." *With that, he tosses the guitar through a gap in the bridge housing as he raises the pistol toward his head. I spring at that exact moment, catching him at the hip as Scoop and McFadden lunge, taking all of us into a tangled heap on the floor of the bridge. Scoop wrestles the gun from his grip as McFadden pins Billy Brad's left arm.*

* * *

Billy Brad confessed to killing D'Amboise. It had been premeditated. Scoop thought it was probable that D'Amboise had been in town initially to scout out the prospects of a scam involving the Roosevelts. After asking around, he had soon discovered the family had no real connection to the museum.

The police interview with Joyce Favor answered a lot of questions. She had dismissed D'Amboise when he approached her by telling him a good lawyer and a DNA test would settle the matter.

His hopes dashed, D'Amboise took notice of Charlene's talent, flattered her, and, with lies about his connection with the music industry, had filled her head with false hope and hatched a plan to make her a star. Billy Brad had thought that if he eliminated the threat, he could persuade Charlene to remain in Warm Springs. Failing that, without D'Amboise in the picture, Billy Brad would be the one to go to Nashville with her.

The staging had been as Scoop and his team thought. It had been an attempt by Billy Brad to misdirect the investigation. The fact that a member of the Roosevelt family was staying at the bed and breakfast had made it a logical ploy.

Scoop decided he would leave the case of Rousso's murder in the capable hands of the Pine Mountain police chief. His time in Warm Springs was done. He looked at his watch. The time limit to cancel his trip to Cancun had passed. There was only one more thing he needed to do before he headed back to Atlanta.

He found Clay in the break room where Birdie and McFadden were packing up their equipment and dismantling the incident room.

"A word," Scoop said to Clay.

The policeman took a step back, a wary expression on his face. "About what?"

"Hannah Sanderson."

Clay shrugged. "What about her?"

"When a woman says no, she means no."

"I don't know what you're talking about." Clay's expression changed to one of affront.

"Sure you do. Billy Brad told me."

"I don't know what Billy Brad said but whatever it is, it's a lie."

With that, Scoop swung with all his might catching Clay on the left cheek. The blow caused him to stumble back into the row of filing cabinets.

Clay's hands went up in a defensive posture. "What the hell!"

"The powerline. You cut it. You were preying on her fear, thinking she would run to you." Scoop shook his right hand against the pain from the blow. "Don't ever go near her or Teagan again."

* * *

Hannah was loading wet swimsuits and towels into the washer when she heard the car. She went to the back door and saw Scoop walking across the lawn. A little flutter bubbled up in her chest. She tamped it back down and opened the back door as he came up the steps.

Teagan had heard the approach of the car, too. She and Fergus came running from her room, anxious to hear all the details of the arrest.

Over warm chocolate chip cookies and milk, Scoop delivered a version of the facts that were best suited for a child. Hannah had already heard all the details from Birdie.

"I still can't believe Billy Brad killed Charlene," Hannah said. "He was in love with her and no one knew."

"They kept it quiet. That was probably her idea. She didn't want any attachments that would interfere with her career. Jolene had seen them together. A couple of her regulars at the beauty shop had commented on seeing them as well. Her death wasn't intentional. He has a temper, apparently. She was threatening to confess what she knew about D'Amboise's death. He lashed out and the blow was fatal."

"Such a tragedy."

"Try to put it behind you. I think there'll be a shake-up at the police department. I heard that Clay is thinking of looking for a job with the Atlanta police department."

"Really?"

Scoop shrugged.

"Because he was part of the big case?" Teagan asked.

"I imagine that had something to do with it," Scoop replied.

"Do you have another murder to solve?" she wanted to know.

"Not at the moment. I think I'm due a little holiday."

"Fishing in Cancun," Hannah said.

Scoop shook his head. "Not this time. My trip got cancelled."

"You could go fishing with us," Teagan said.

"Are you a big fisherman?" he asked.

"Mr. Wilkes taught me."

"Then I imagine you're pretty good at it."

She smiled. "There's a contest at the Memorial Day picnic."

"Is there?"

"You could come."

Scoop looked from Teagan to Hannah. "Maybe I will."

Chapter Thirty-Two

The Farmer's Wife made pancakes for breakfast this morning. Usually she's a biscuit person. Or rather, The Farmer is. I think she did it because she knows Dax is leaving today.

He seems more relaxed this morning. I suppose being suspected of murder does tend to make one tense. But now he's free to roam about the country. I wonder where his next adventure will take him. Things will be awfully dull around here after all the excitement of triple murders.

I walk with him to the intersection of the train tracks and Broad Street. The train will slow to a crawl here for the sake of safety. He confided last night that he thought he'd travel by rail to his next stop. It doesn't seem to matter whether the train is going east or west, just so it's going somewhere. A life of adventure, that's my man Dax.

In the distance I hear the faint hum of the rails. After a bit,

Dax hears it too. The train is coming out of the west.

He looks down at me. "This'll be my ride," *he says.* "I guess you'll keep the law in Warm Springs now. You're pretty good at it."

I am pretty good at it. But I doubt there'll be much excitement for quite some time. The town is exhausted with the happenings of the past week. There's always Lil the Librarian. She likes an audience when she reads, especially if it's a thriller or a horror story. Then there's the usual rounds. Boring stuff, actually.

Dax's backpack sits on the ground at his feet. He's off on a new adventure. I look up at him and climb into the open pouch on top.

He studies me a minute. "You do know I'm about to hop this train, don't you?"

I settle more deeply into the opening in the backpack created by the frame of his lightweight pup tent.

"Life on the road isn't all fried fish and blueberry cobbler, you know."

I look at him and blink.

He hesitates a moment. "All right then, but you have to keep up. I don't hold with slackers."

As if I would ever be considered a slacker!

He swings the backpack onto his shoulders, me gripping with my claws, and he begins to jog as the train comes alongside us. An open box car appears and with deft movements he swings up into the opening. We are on our way.

I climb out of the backpack and lean out the opening, watching Warm Springs become a small dot in the distance. I probably should have said goodbye to Lil. And to Trudy and The Farmer's Wife. Not The Farmer. He won't miss me at all.